THE

NEWB

THE ADVENTURES OF HORC:

BOOK 1

BY DREW SEREN

See what Drew Seren is up to.
Visit his website www.drewseren.com
And sign up for his newsletter

Copyright 2018 © MysticHawker Press
http://www.mystichawker.com/

ISBN: 13- 978-1-945632-32-7

Edited by Robert Bronson
Cover design by Anadia-chan
www.anadia-chan.com

1

ALAN GOSLING stared at the clock on his phone. One more minute and he'd be free for the weekend. After a week of group meetings intermingled with endless hours of tech support calls for people who had very little idea of how to use their haptic pods, he was ready to walk away for a couple of days and throw himself into his own pod and enjoy hours of roaming the galaxy in Galactic Explorers. One of the benefits of working for Total Immersion Systems was discounts on the latest and greatest gaming tech. Sure, he'd rewired his house to meet the power requirements of the pod, but it had been worth it. The difference between the pod experience and inky using a VR helmet and gloves was amazing.

When his phone flashed six o'clock, Alan hit the button to take him out of the queue, logged off his computer, grabbed his messenger bag and dashed for the door. He hoped no one would call out to him, needing his help with a difficult call. As a floor lead, he'd be required to stop and lend a hand, but he made it to the elevator without issue.

Alan tapped the button to head to the tram stop that ran through the building, one floor below street level.

"Hold the elevator!" Mike Simmons, one of the guys on Alan's team, came rushing down the hall. He looked like he was as happy to get away from the place for the weekend as Alan was.

Alan pressed the button to hold the door, and Mike slid in, huffing like a steam engine. Even the short dash had been more than his out-of-shape body was used to.

"Thanks, Alan." Mike wheezed. "Man, I wish game time had the same physical benefits as real life; unfortunately real life isn't as cool."

"That's one way to look at it," Alan agreed. He did his best to find a balance between time in his pod and time down in the gym down the block in his housing complex. But even so, he wasn't in the same shape as he'd been in his twenties. He'd been thinking about trying some of the new fitness add-ons for the pod that incorporated neural stimulation with his game, although since he spent most of his time in-game on the bridge of a starship as Captain Malfoy, he wasn't sure that would be much help.

"Hey, what do you think of the new beta the designers want us to test out?" Mike asked.

"Another fantasy game," Alan said, trying to hide his dislike for Elves, Dwarves and the like. He'd played a few fantasy games back in college before the pods came along and changed gaming forever, but he'd always found science fiction games so much more interesting.

"Yeah, but the company's offering a sweet bonus for the beta testers." As the elevator came to a stop and the doors opened, Mike put his hand out and held the door while Alan walked out. "Honestly, I probably wouldn't be doing it, if it weren't for the cash. My wife has a fit if I spend too much time in-world."

"One of the benefits of being single," Alan said. "My time is mine." He hadn't heard about the testing bonus. He could always use some extra cash. "Is the information on the website? To be honest, I zoned out the rest of the meeting when they started talking about that game….what was it called?"

"Halfworld," Mike supplied as they walked toward the group of people waiting for the tram. "Sure, it's a fantasy world, but it's all about the choices you make that impact how the world interacts with you. I read up on it after the meeting."

"In between phone calls?" Alan already knew the answer, a lot of his team, himself included often entertained themselves online while they were talking with customers, particularly when it was something they'd heard many, many times.

"Sure. But anyway, there're two factions, like a lot of games, but you can opt to go in between factions, so it opens up the whole world as opposed to just the parts your faction controls. The catch is, depending on how you play, you can lose your neutrality, or if you're playing a faction, change factions. Can't say as I've encountered anything like that before." Mike paused as the tram arrived and everyone crowded on.

Alan waited until the tram was moving to continue talking after he and Mike got seats next to each other. He still wasn't overly interested in a fantasy game, but for extra money at work, he could beta test it. He wondered how much paperwork would be involved if he did it. "But it's still Elves, Dwarves, Humans and such?"

"Yeah, but apparently you can also mix up the races too."

"Like a Half-Elf, Half-Dwarf?" Alan tried to picture what that would look like. It had probably been a challenge for the coders to come up with the body types.

"Yeah, or something that's half and half between factions. Elves and Dwarves are on the same side." Mike's phone rang and he answered it.

Alan looked out the window. Dark clouds looked like they were bearing in from the west. Fort Worth was probably already getting hit with a storm. It felt like it had rained all week in Dallas and, from the look of the sky, it wasn't likely to stop anytime soon.

Mike ended his call. "Sorry. The wife. She needs me to stop by the store at the tram stop and pick up a few things before I get home. So anyway, I'm going to roll up my toon tonight and get started. If you want, I can send you a text when I get done and we can see about running together. That'll make things easier. I'm good at fantasy games, and if we're partied up, I can make sure you don't look like a total newb."

"I've played fantasy games before," Alan replied. He wasn't sure he liked the way Mike was assuming he'd jump right into the game and be a complete moron about it.

"But your thing is Galactic Explorers." Mike nodded. "I totally understand having a perfered genre, but trust me, this is going to be fun."

The tram stopped and Mike stood. "My stop. I'll text you later."

"Okay." Alan pulled out his phone and logged onto the company website the second Mike was walking down the aisle. He almost felt like he was going to be doing extra work on his free time, but it was a game, and if he got paid for testing it, he'd be fine with that.

He found the page he needed and he scanned down the information about the beta testing. It had started earlier that day and would continue for another six months. They wanted weekly reports, in-game, about the experience, but beyond that, they weren't asking for much, and if the tester lasted for six months, playing at least four hours a week, there was a five-thousand-dollar bonus in it. Five grand wasn't much, but it was something Alan could use. He started filling out the participation form and was so engrossed in it, he nearly missed his stop.

AS LIGHTNING danced outside his window, Alan eased himself into his pod.It closed over him, cutting off most exterior stimulus. The system would provide for his bodily needs until he was finished with the game. Some of the customers he spoke to on the phone found their first few times in the pods very claustrophobic, but he hadn't, not even during his initial game. Since then, he'd used it so often with Galactic Explorers that he was used to it. He'd downloaded Halfworld into the pod and set it as the game he wanted to run. He linked his phone to the pod's communications system, so when Mike texted, he'd know and could respond. As his pod kicked in, it blocked out the lingering sounds of the world beyond. The rumble of thunder and traffic died down. The music from his neighbor's weekly Friday party vanished.

Alan sighed heavily as the simple pleasure of being in the pod sank in. For a few moments, there was nothing. He was all by himself. The faint lights he'd turned down before entering the pod were barely visible through the window in the pod's lid. Then everything went dark.

A splash screen filled his vision. It was his first time in Halfworld. He needed to create a toon. Since he was just doing it for a few extra bucks, he didn't expect to keep up with the game after the six required months, so he did something he'd never done before in a game. He hit random on most screens that popped up for basic character creation.

Before him stood a male Half Orc. It was a big hulking brute, but not as massive as an Orc would be. Its skin was a mid-tone green, and its hair was black atop his broad forehead. The faintest hint of white tusks stuck out of a human-looking mouth. He wore leather armor and carried a bow with a short sword strapped to his hip.

There was even a tribal tattoo on his upper arm. Across the top the screen read **Ranger**.

Alan nodded to himself. He could handle a Ranger. If Halfworld was like earlier fantasy games he'd played, the Ranger would be a good in-between class. It would be rough and steady if things came to hand-to-hand combat, but would also be skilled at distance attacks with the bow. It would be a decent class to just run around in the game for a while. It might even be fun.

A window popped up prompting Alan to apply stat points. He had the base points the Half Orc started with, but he had additional points he could use to modify the toon to his own personal likes.

Strength 12
Intelligence 9
Stamina 11
Constitution 13
Charisma 8
Dexterity 9

He had ten additional points he could allot wherever he wanted. Alan didn't think that Rangers relied too much on their Charisma, and being Half Orc probably accounted for the low number there. He wasn't hideous, but not attractive either. If he played the toon right, he could overcome a low Charisma score just by his interactions with other characters. He left that one alone.

He added two points to his Strength and his Constitution. Doing so, he increased his damage and his hit points. He didn't want the character to have trouble with tasks like reading, or deciphering, so he added two points to his Intelligence. He took a second and checked what the Stamina and Dexterity would do for him, although he was fairly sure he knew. Raising his Stamina by one would help him regenerate hit points and also aid him in physical tasks that required endurance. The last three points he put into his Dexterity. It would help him avoid hits and survive things like falls while making it easier for him to climb.

Alan studied his new toon, feeling fairly good about what he'd done. He'd created a well-rounded character that should be fun to run, depending on how the game played out.

The name box was empty. The cursor flashed there, obviously waiting for him to enter something. Alan looked at the box for random, like he'd done with most of the rest of the toon. Nothing happened. He tried tapping on it, but nothing happened. With a frustrated sigh, Alan stared at the character. "Who are you?"

The character's race caught his attention. Half Orc. He wasn't about to just name it Half Orc. That would be stupid. "Horc," Alan muttered. "You're Horc."

The letters appeared on the screen.

Alan nodded. "Alright. Let's play this game." He focused his attention on the accept button. The splash screen vanished and everything flashed black.

2

HORC STOOD on a dark dais encircled with torches that were just out of reach. The light from the torches didn't reach far. Horc couldn't tell if he was in a room, or outdoors, but the fact that the torches burned straight up and didn't flicker, seemed to hint that he was in a room of some sort. Before he could call out, a window appeared, floating just above him.

The letters were yellow against a black background.

Horc the Ranger, you are a Half Orc, as such, you stand between two races, currently loved by neither, but similarly hated by neither as well. As such, you must choose which side of your heritage you wish to embrace first. Which starting area would you prefer to begin your questing in?

Below the question, two buttons appeared, they glowed yellow like the text. One indicated **Human**, while the other read **Orc**.

Horc stared at the question for a moment. He hadn't heard from Mike. He had no idea which zone his friend was going to start in. The choice wasn't one he'd anticipated. He'd never played a half-breed before. The question made Horc wish he'd spent time studying a manual or something, but since they were beta testing the game, there wasn't any kind of manual or forum he could consult to make an informed decision. He figured if he'd rolled up some other half combo, his choices of starting zones would be different.

"Human," Horc said impulsively.

The flames on the torches suddenly guttered and then blew out. When the darkness cleared again, Horc stood in the center of the large courtyard. Around him, various people hurried around the area. Most of them appeared human, although there were short humanoids with long beards, willowy humanoids with pointed ears, and some things that didn't appear overly humanoid at all, but more insect and animal.

"Welcome, Horc the Ranger," a large man in a guard's uniform drew Horc's attention from the other people in the stone courtyard. Above his head, green text with gold border read **Stone Helm City Guard Level XXX**

Horc stared at the man. He held a large axe with a sword belted to his armored waist. He was covered head to toe in plate armor. But he was the closest guard to Horc, so Horc assumed he was the guard who'd spoken.

"Greetings," Horc said, doing his best to sound jovial. He had no idea how seriously the AI controlling the game was going to take its interactions with the players. "Do you happen to know where I can find the first quest I need to do?"

The guard nodded. "You're new here. I can send you to Caleb Sureshot, the Ranger trainer who is in Druid Park near the center of the city."

A box appeared above the guard's head.

Quest: Find Caleb Sureshot
Ranger Special Quest
Rewards 100 XP

This time the buttons showed **Accept** and **Decline**.

Horc grinned. "Accept."

The box disappeared.

"I've put a spot on your map to show you where to find Sureshot," the guard said. "Remember, Horc, we watch your kind around here." The information above his head was no longer ringed in gold. It was just simple green text.

Not exactly sure what he was talking about, Horc gave him a slight bow. "I'll behave myself, I promise."

"Be sure that you do." The guard slipped his axe onto his back, and crossed his arms, obviously dismissing Horc.

Wondering about the guard's warning, Horc pursed his lips, then noticed a small flashing green light in the upper left of his vision. He tapped the light and a small map appeared. It showed the streets and buildings of the town. Stone Helm City was in big letters across the top of the map. If the blue arrow on the edge of the city was his location, the red dot in the green area near the center of the city was logically the trainer he was supposed to go find.

Horc pushed against the edge of the map, making it smaller in his field of view, but not so small that it was difficult to read and he took off toward Druid Park. He stared at the city as he walked around. It reminded him of a German city he'd been to during a tour of Europe several years earlier. The cobblestone streets were fairly narrow, but full of people. In addition to the races Horc had seen already, there were Centaurs, and something he couldn't name that were short with bulbous noses and huge ears. They all had green text over their heads, indicating their names and in some cases, such as the wandering bread merchant, their profession. At one point there was something going on in one of the streets, and a bunch of the NPCs were gathered there. With so many of them standing together like that, Horc had trouble telling one from another. There was a lot of yelling, and guards were trying to get through the mob, or at least Horc assumed they were guards, based on their armor that looked exactly like the guard he'd spoken to. He didn't see any point to standing there gawking; it wasn't like the disturbance would mean anything to him. But it was interesting that the game would include things like that in its interface. Horc pressed on toward Druid Park.

He was nearly there, when a chime sounded around him and a box popped up on the lower left side of his vision.

Incoming text.
Accept-Decline?

Hoping it was Mike, Horc swiped 'Accept.'

Hey, I'm in. Are you in yet? Where are you? Who are you?

Stone Helm City, heading toward Druid Park. I'm Horc. Alan replied, speaking slowly and the words appeared in the text box.

Another box popped up.

Baladara invites you to a party.
Accept–Decline.

Cool. Accept the party invite and I'll find you, Mike responded.

Horc swiped 'Accept.'

Another dot appeared on his map. This one was blue and back near the guard. Below the map was the head shot of what looked like an elven female with blonde hair. There were two stat bars below the image.

The text box disappeared and another box appeared. It had 'Party Chat' across the top.

'Okay. This is easier.' appeared in blue text in the chat box next to the name Baladara.

Yes, it is. Horc replied. His text appeared in white.

Good. I'm going to run to the Mage trainer. I guess you're going to the Druid trainer. Baladara

Ranger. Horc replied as he walked across a small flat bridge that spanned a swiftly running stream. A quick glance showed the stream wasn't a pristine fantasy stream, but looked like what he'd expect a medieval stream in the middle of a town to look like, with lots of gunk, and smelly items floating around in it. There was even a slight stench to it. Horc knew he'd give points to the game designers for incorporating that. He liked his games as real as possible; that's why he preferred to play science fiction games.

Cool. You can defend my scrawny mage ass until I'm high enough level to do a ton of damage. Baladara

So, do you want to find me, or should I find you? Horc asked as he made a turn as his map indicated.

Let's just meet at the main gate. We'll probably have the same starting quest anyway. Baladara

Okay. Let's try to get there quickly.

Sure. See you soon. Baladara

On the map, Baladara's blue dot headed toward a building labeled **Mage Tower**.

Horc continued toward Druid Park. He stopped in his tracks when the stone buildings of the city gave way to a thick forest. He'd expected something like the city parks of Dallas, not the primal density of the Black Forest in Europe. As he walked into the trees, heading toward the dot on his map, the background sounds of the city fell away. He couldn't hear the barkers calling out their wares, or the horses pulling wagons across cobblestone streets. It was replaced by birdsong and squirrel chatter.

Near the center of the park, the trees opened up into a pleasant grove. Several green and brown fabric tents stood around the edge of the grove. A large fire occupied its center. There were five NPCs spaced out around the fire.

One of the NPCs, a tall man with a nasty-looking bow slung over his shoulder, grinned and walked toward Horc. The sword at his waist swung with each step. A massive black wolf paced at his side. "Greetings, Horc. Why have you sought me out this day?"

The text over his head was green tinged in yellow. It read **Caleb Sureshot Ranger XXX**

"I have come to begin my training," Horc replied.

"Good." Caleb's grin widened and he reached down to stroke the head of the wolf who'd sat next to him.

A box popped up.

Quest: Find Caleb Sureshot – completed.
Reward 100 XP
Reputation with Humans +10
Reputation with Rangers +50

"The way of the Ranger is a good one for half-breeds of all kinds," Sureshot began. "Like the Druids, we stand at the points between light and dark. We answer to the green. To further this, we do what we must to keep the balance in our world."

"I understand," Horc said.

"Good. To that end, I task you with a simple quest. Go into the forest beyond the city. Find the herd of swine that has taken up residence on the eastern edge near the river. We believe that minions of the Gnoll king are forcing them this way in his efforts to disrupt the true path of nature. The swine are destroying the forest where they dwell. Slay ten of them and come back to me."

A box popped up

Quest: Swine Hunt
Objectives kill ten swine east of the city
Rewards 300 xp, Forest cloak, 25 copper
Accept-Decline

Killing pigs sounded easy. Horc accepted the quest.

"Very good. I'll see you when you have succeeded." The yellow aura around Sureshot's name disappeared.

Horc glanced at his map. Baladara's blue dot was still at the Mage Tower. He had a new arrow on the map. It was silver and pointed out the city gate. Since the map was only of the city, Horc wondered if the arrow was going to change to a dot when he left the city and was nearing the quest location. If it had been Galactic Explorer, he'd have had a dotted line appearing on the map showing him where he needed to go, which stargates he needed to use, et cetera, but he was new to fantasy gaming in general and Halfworld in particular. He was going to do it all without much of a clue.

As he left Druid Park behind, Baladara's dot left the Mage Tower and started toward the main gate. After the quiet of Druid Park, the noise of the people in the city was a bit much. Horc wished he had a way to dampen the sounds, but that would take away from the immersive experience the pods provided. Most people wanted as real an experience as possible.

Nearing the gate, Horc slowed. Baladara's dot was still a short distance away. He stepped into a small shop a few doors down from the stone wall that indicated the edge of the city. The place was dimly lit with three people standing in it. Two were NPC with green text over their heads. The other was a player. His text was blue and declared him to be **Mordred, Witch, level two**.

"Greetings, Sir Ranger," the burly man behind the counter said. "Welcome to my armory. What can I help you with?"

The player turned. "Cool, another play…" His eyes got large. "What's an Orc doing in Stone Helm and why are you showing as friendly?" He pulled his sword. "Is this a glitch? I'll report it."

Horc held up empty hands. "Whoa there. I'm a Half-Orc, not a full Orc. Neutral." Horc wondered how he'd feel in Galactic Explorers if he ran into someone from a slaver race claiming to be neutral. He'd probably shoot the guy and worry about it later.

Mordred frowned. "Half-Orc? Was that even an option? I thought this was going to be fairly basic play. Neutral? That's a new one on me. You better be careful out there. Some of the guys aren't going to wait for you to say anything. Honestly, if we'd met in the forest, I'd just run you through. This is a PVP server after all."

"I hear you." Horc glanced around the shop. A fair number of staves hung on the wall behind the counter that was full of wands and other things he couldn't exactly identify, but figured they were magical weapons of one form or another. There were also cloaks, and other cloth gear. Somehow, since he was spawned with a bow and a short sword, he'd most likely be better served in a different shop.

"See you all around." Horc walked out of the shop as Baladara's dot drew close enough he should be coming around the next corner at any moment.

A willowy elf female came bouncing around the corner. Blue text with a slight silver aura declared her to be **Baladara, Mage, level one**.

"Oh, wow, Alan?" Baladara stopped and stared. "Dude, do you always go ugly on your toons?"

Horc shook his head. "Me? Mike, do you always play women?"

Baladara bounced up and down causing her breasts to bounce. "It beats looking at my ugly mug while I'm playing." She spun around on one foot, her blonde hair streaming out around her. "Come on, don't you want to date my avatar?"

"No." Horc shook his head again. "Does your wife know you play females?"

"Sure. She even helps me design them. When she plays, she likes to run dudes. Sometimes she even strips them naked…and I mean all the way. Due to some hacks, she used to see everything. She says she likes to think they might be what I could look like if I cared to make myself better for her."

Horc had known other guys who liked to run female toons, but that had been mostly before the pods became popular. Most guys in the pods came up with the best versions of themselves they could. "Oh, you're still using VR, not immersion, aren't you?"

Baladara shrugged. "Wife and kid. I can't afford the high dollar stuff, not even with a company discount. Not to mention, if I plopped a pod down in the living room, my wife would shoot me."

"Got it. So what quest did you get?"

"Pig killing. I need to bring back eight hooves that can be used in spells."

"Oookaayy." Horc shook his head. "I've just got to kill them. If our grouping works out, by the time I get all the ones I need, you'll have the parts your quest requires."

Baladara grinned. "It's partying but sounds good to me. Let's go kill ourselves some swine." She bounced again and headed for the gate.

As Horc walked alongside her while she jumped and skipped her way out the city, he wondered how many levels they'd be able to get their first night, and how pissed Mike would be if he did some leveling without him.

3

THE LAND outside the city walls was rolling forest. A dirt road ran toward the south. For a short distance, there weren't any trees, but when they started, they had an almost park-like feel to them. Very few were bushy, reaching down to the ground, but had a trimmed look, like someone had gone in with a chainsaw and taken all the lower limbs off to make it easier for players to walk through the forest.

"Wow, this looks pretty good," Baladara said as they walked. "They look like real trees and everything. The company put a lot of effort into giving an authentic feeling to everything."

"Yeah, very Earthlike," Horc agreed. He glanced at the map in the upper left of his vision. Although there weren't any details there, for things like roads, streams, mountains, and other landmarks, there was a glowing yellow dot off a short distance east of the road.

"Hey, you should lighten up on the fantasy versus science fiction thing," Baladara said. "We're getting paid to have fun in this world, let's have some fun."

Horc wasn't about to admit he'd made more than a few comparisons to his beloved Galactic Explorers. But he didn't see any way to not make the comparisons. It was what he had experience with; the only time he'd played a fantasy game, it hadn't gone well. "I'll try. It's all fairly new to me."

"All I can ask is that you try." Baladara stopped and got a faraway look. "I think we need to head off that way." She pointed to the east, in the direction of the yellow dot on the map.

Horc nodded. "Looks that way."

"Okay. Well, stay on your guard. Most fantasy MMORPGs have settings so that chance encounters with mobs are higher when you leave the roads." Baladara shook out her hands as they walked across the green grass toward the tree line. She looked like a gunslinger getting ready for a fight.

"Mobs are the bad guys, right?" Horc didn't normally run with other characters. The crew of his starship were all non-player characters who he'd recruited as parts of quests and occasional drops from bosses he'd killed.

"Yeah, although I tend to think of them as mobs when there are more than one. For some reason, calling a single monster or bad guy a mob just doesn't sound right, even if a lot of people do," Baladara replied. "But be on guard, this game is totally new territory. We've got no idea what to expect. If I were you, I'd keep either your bow or your sword in your hand at all times when you're off the roads."

A squirrel ran across the ground between two trees. As Horc targeted it, yellow text above it declared it to be **Squirrel level one**.

Baladara stopped and flexed her hands.

"Wait a minute," Horc said. "Dude, it's a squirrel."

The little pixel varmint scampered up a tree.

"Yeah, but I bet it's worth XP, at least at this level." Baladara made series of circular gestures that made her hands glow, then thrust her index finger toward the squirrel's tail as it disappeared around the back of the tree. A bolt of blue light flew from her finger and struck the tree. Bark rained down.

"Damn. Missed." Baladara brushed her hands together. "But you normally miss your first shot... or three. At least this was just a squirrel and not one of the pigs we need for the quest."

Horc kept walking toward the yellow dot on the map. "I think, unless there's more in it than XP, I'll skip killing squirrels."

"Then don't blame me when I level faster than you." Baladara let out a sigh and resumed walking next to him.

"I promise I won't." Horc said as they came to a small creek cutting through the forest.

The water was a lot cleaner than the stream in town had been. There was a soft bubbling sound to it, and there were fish swimming around in the clear depths. Horc stopped and stooped down next to it. He was surprised at his reflection in the water. It looked just like it had when he'd rolled up the toon, but just seeing it in the water was a detail he hadn't expected from the game.

"The details are amazing." Horc dipped his hands into the water and scooped out some water and dribbled it into his mouth. It even tasted like clean spring water.

A green **+1** appeared in his vision and his mana bar flashed.

Horc straightened and stared at Baladara. "Hey, did it just try to improve my mana? And I'm a Ranger, what do I need mana for anyway?"

"Just for drinking from the creek?" Baladara knelt down and drank a bit, then grinned. "Cool. That replenished the mana I used shooting the squirrel. Normally you need a mana potion or some other kind of drink you can get from either a wandering vendor or an inn keeper. I wonder if we can buy refillable containers like canteens. That would be awesome."

"Okay. So the creek water is cool. But why does a Ranger need mana?" Horc hopped across the creek and continued toward the yellow dot.

Baladara hurried to keep up. "I'm not totally sure in Halfworld, but in other games, Rangers, Hunters, and the like can have spells they use with their attacks, like flaming arrows, and that sort of thing. You might also get some kind of animal control. Did you read the description before selecting the class?"

Horc angled around a large boulder that looked out of place on the hill that was gently sloping upward. "Nope. Not really planning on playing this game beyond the paid time, and just used random on most everything when I was rolling the toon."

"Really?" Baladara laughed. "You've got to be kidding me. You don't play fantasy games so you just randomed everything? You could've gotten stuck with a dwarf thief or something else lame like that. You never, never just random your character. I guess that explains the Half-Orc thing you've got going on. At least it will be a bit of a challenge."

"Yeah, I've already scared the pants off some Witch back in town. Okay, can you explain to me the difference between a Witch and a Mage?"

"Witches are a bit harder to run, at least that what the minimal wiki we have available said. They are a lot more dependent on spell components. They use things to cast their spells and it takes them less mana to do it. A Mage doesn't need bits of wool, feathers, tree bark and stuff, but it takes us more mana. I mean, I guess it does balance out in a fashion, but I don't want to have to keep up with the various stuff in my bags." Baladara came to a spot and pointed. "Looks like our first pig."

A couple of trees in front of them, a small bristly pig rooted near the base of a tree. It was even grunting as it did. Horc targeted it and above it appeared yellow text **Young Forest Pig level 1**.

"Does it matter which one of us hits it first?" Horc asked as he unslung his bow before reaching back into his quiver for an arrow. As he did, he realized he hadn't listened to Baladara and had his sword in hand as they walked through the forest. He couldn't decide if that was a good thing, or a potential disaster.

"We're partied, so it shouldn't matter. We share the kills, while splitting the XP and loot." Baladara's hands glowed and a magical bolt of light flew from them and hit the pig. A health bar appeared under the pig's text, which turned red. A quarter of the health dropped as the pig jerked its head up, squealed and rushed them.

Horc fired an arrow. It hit the pig and the creature's health dropped to a little under half.

Baladara got off another bolt of magic, and it only had a quarter of its health left. Then Horc's second arrow hit it.

The pig stopped, shuddered and fell over as its health bar blinked and disappeared.

White text appeared in the middle of Horc's view.

1 swine of 10

Experience: 25 points

Reward: Hog flank

Baladara stared at the corpse and huffed. "No hooves. Just my luck. What do you want to bet we have to kill dozens of these things to get the eight hooves I need? I'll never understand how creatures don't drop body part loot that would be essential to their survival. How do pigs run without hooves? And if they run with hooves, why don't we get 4 hooves for every pig we kill?"

"Maybe only perfect hooves count?" Horc said with a shrug. At that point it didn't make much difference to him if they had hooves or not. He got points for killing.

"What?" Baladara glared at Horc, then a thoughtful line crossed her forehead. "You know, that might be it. The idea is stupid, but that might be the answer. Players have been wondering about that for years."

"Maybe we can point that out in our beta report," Horc said as he looked around in the forest for another pig to target. "To help make things clearer to players, maybe they can change the quest parameters to read 'perfect hooves' as opposed to just 'hooves', so folks understand what they're going after."

Baladara laughed. "You really do over-think things, don't you? I'm constantly amazed that you've never made manager, but then you care about helping people too much, and not just worry about call times and such."

"That's me," Horc said, then gestured with his bow as another pig shuffled into view. **Young Forest Pig level 1** "Next target acquired."

"Too sci-fi, Dude, too sci-fi."

Horc didn't reply. He fired his bow and the arrow streaked across the distance and hit the pig. Its squeal sounded more angry than hurt as it charged them. Its health bar wasn't down much.

"We need to work on your crits." Baladara unleashed her spell that hit the pig and dropped it below half.

"Is there a way to work on those, or is it just the AI?" Horc shot another arrow and the final bit of the pig's health dropped as the pig collapsed at their feet.

His screen flashed.

2 swine of 10

Experience: 25 points

"Hey, there's a hoof!" Baladara cheered as she bent down and retrieved the loot. "Only seven more to go!"

"Then let's keep killing these guys." Horc nocked another arrow. "I don't know why I figured there'd be more of them clustered around or something."

Baladara shook her head as she placed the hoof in her bag. "Not always. Sometimes things work like that, but don't count on it. Like the hoof drops."

They quickly found more pigs and the creatures went down with three to four hits. Horc was just getting a pig targeted when a loud squeal come from off to the left.

"This one!" Baladara yelled. "It's a level three." She hit it with a spell and kept her hands going to get more spells off.

Horc stared for a second at the text above the pig rampaging toward them. It was red and read **Forest Pig level 3**

"Shoot it already!" Baladara continued to get off spells. Her mana bar was dropping quickly and the pig slammed into her, sending her flying into a tree.

"Crap." Horc fired an arrow. It hit the pig whose health only about a quarter of the way down.

Baladara continued to cast spells as her mana bar began to flash red. Her health bar dropped with each attack from the beast.

Horc fired three more arrows, and the pig was down to half health. When he reached back for another arrow, his quiver was empty. "I'm out of arrows."

"Out of arrows?" Baladara sounded incredulous. "How can you be out of arrows? Didn't you buy some before leaving town?"

"Buy arrows? I have to buy arrows?" Horc dropped his bow and pulled his sword. "Why do I have to buy arrows?"

His first hit with the sword caused the pig to turn and face him. Its health was a bit under half, but they'd had to do a lot to it to get it that low.

"Arrows aren't free. You had your starter set and that's it. After that you have to buy arrows." Baladara attacked the pig one last time with magic, then her mana bar went dark. She pulled out a knife.

"It's not like my laser then." When the pig's tusk raked Horc's side, he wanted to scream in pain.

A message flashed in red on his screen as his health bar slid to the left. **-10**

The pain made him wonder if the game's interface settings were too high. He'd never felt agony like that in another game. He hit the pig in the head with the pommel of his sword, driving it to its knees. It raked its tusks into his thigh.

Horc swung his sword around and drove it point down into the pig's shoulder.

His screen flashed. **Critical hit +50 damage**

The pig's health bar flashed red, then vanished as it collapsed on the ground.

7 swine out of 10
Experience: 60 points
Reward:
Broken Tusk
Hog shank

"At least the damned thing has another hoof," Baladara said. "You keep the tusk and shank." She put the hoof in her bag then sat down next to the pig's corpse. "Too bad neither one of us is a healer, or has cooking or skinning."

Horc put the rest of the loot in his bag. "Okay. I understand the healer, but cooking or skinning?" He still hurt from his wounds and sat next to Baladara, wondering how long it was going to take for his health to get back to normal so the pain would stop.

Baladara sighed and pulled out a flask and drank from it. Instantly her mana bar began rising. "I'm betting you didn't get any food before we left town."

Horc shook his head. "I didn't check on the price of food, but I've only got a few copper pieces on me. I figured I'd get some loot and sell it before worrying about things like food."

"We're getting pig meat. If either one of us had cooking, we could make a meal of it and help our health get back to normal faster." Baladara pulled her backpack off and set it in front of her. "We don't have much yet, so we might not be able to get food, or more than a few arrows. We'll have to see what the prices are like."

"And skinning?"

"Skinning is one of the several in game professions we can get. Well, we can only have two professions, so choose carefully. Most rangers get skinning, herb gathering, gardening, things like that so you can make extra cash from kills. Take a look at this pig. Under the name it shows 'skinnable,' now that it's dead. I bet things lower than level three aren't skinnable, because I haven't seen that before."

"So how do we get professions?" Horc's own health bar was nearly full again.

"We go to trainers once we're high enough level. We'll need to either check with the wiki, or see when we get the option as we level. Most games it's level five to ten."

"So it's like schooling in a science fiction game." Horc watched the pig turn pale, then translucent before finally fading completely from view. "You're in the academy for whichever course you want to take, then once you clear a few levels you can spread things out, going to see the universe, or joining the space marines."

"Sort of, but you really need to get into a fantasy mindset. Totally different thing." Baladara took a final draw from her flask and it vanished. Her mana bar was full, and her health was nearly three quarters. "Alright. I've got four more hooves to get, and you've got three more pigs to kill. Let's try and avoid these big mommas for a little while, at least until we're level two."

Horc stood. His health bar was back to full. "Why until we're level two?"

"Because level twos hit harder than level ones." Baladara shook her head. "Really, it's a sword and a bow, not a ray gun."

"I'll get the hang of it." Horc walked over and picked up his bow and slung it over his shoulder. "Until we get back to town, it's sword only for me."

"Yep. One big plus to being a caster is you can renew your mana easier, unless you're a Witch and need spell components. Let's knock these guys down, and get going so we can get you some arrows. I hope we can level before we head back to town. Putting on a couple of levels tonight would be nice. I hate starting a new character who stays low for too long." Baladara brushed herself off and started off through the forest.

Horc hurried after her. He wanted to put on a level or two before he logged out. Although he was still getting the hang of things, he figured it would get more interesting than just killing pigs fairly quickly.

4

WHEN PIG ten fell, instead of flashing the number of pigs, the message that appeared on Horc's screen announced:

Quest Swine Hunt Complete

A golden glow encircled Horc and the screen flashed gold letters that were nearly three times as large as any previous message **Level 2**

"Hey," Baladara said. "How come you're leveling before I am? That's not fair."

"I wonder if Rangers level faster than Mages." Horc didn't bother opening his character sheet to check out his upgrades for leveling. He was busy looking around for another pig. They still needed two more hooves for Baladara.

"Maybe." Baladara frowned heavily. "I'll ask around and see what people can tell me. It looks like I've only got a few more points to go."

"How can you tell?" Horc asked. It would be nice to be able to tell things like where he was sitting level-wise.

"Look at your avatar up with the party info," Baladara explained. "Tap on the icon there and it'll expand to show your leveling progress bar."

Horc did as he instructed. There was a couple of additional bars including his XP bar, and his reputation bars with the different factions. He was sitting at just off neutral, is separate directions, with both major factions. His reputation with Rangers was growing. "How did you figure all this out?"

"Spent a few minutes tapping and swiping my way around the screen while I was walking to the Mage Tower after I got the first quest from the guard at the gate." Baladara scanned around the area, obviously looking for more pigs, since she still needed two more hooves to finish her quest.

"I never even thought of that. I'm used to getting a personnel report each time I level to let me know how I'm doing." Horc looked around, hoping they could find a few more pigs so he could go turn in his quest.

Suddenly the world shook, and everything became out of focus for a moment.

"What was that?" Horc glanced around as everything seemed to solidify and become crystal clear again.

"Dude, that was weird," Baladara said. "You looked like you lost focus for a few seconds. Like you were about to log off or something."

Horc shook his head. "I wasn't trying to log off. I don't know what happened. So you saw something that was limited to my avatar, and I saw something that seemed to affect the entire game."

"We'd better file a bug report." Baladara tapped the air in front of her. "Go to your main screen. There's a special button in the lower right-hand corner that won't be there after the beta concludes. There's a spider on it. That's your special bug report button."

Horc brought up the window and saw what Baladara was talking about. "If you're reporting it, should I do it too?"

"I figure they'd probably appreciate that since we both saw something different." Baladara's hands moved like she was typing, then swiping through something. "If we give them different points of view for the same phenomena, they can figure out exactly what happened and make sure it doesn't affect too many toons."

"Okay." Horc tapped the spider icon and a form appeared on the screen. A keyboard appeared right below it. Although the keys were at an awkward vertical position to what he was used to when he typed, Horc managed to not take forever filling in the form and submitting it.

Baladara looked like she was done when he closed the window. "Alright, let's get these last hooves."

"Sounds good." Horc pulled his sword from its scabbard, still wishing he'd known about the arrows when he'd been in town. It would be nice to have enough to not abandon the bow even for a little while. He was taking more damage having to run up and hit the pigs with the sword than he'd done when flinging arrows at them. If they got really lucky, there'd only be another couple that they'd need to kill before they headed back to town.

THEY HAD to kill four more pigs to get the last two hooves Baladara needed. She'd leveled after the second one. They headed back to town, with her killing squirrels any time they popped up. It made Horc wonder if there were squirrels of higher level than one. Even so, they didn't attack the way the first-level pigs did, they normally just died and since they were still partied, he got two XP for each one. It didn't seem like a good use of mana, although Baladara didn't seem to mind as she walked along. She was normally back up to full strength by the time she spotted the next squirrel, killed it, and got them both 2 more XP.

At the gate, they parted ways, Baladara heading toward Mage Tower and Horc going toward Druid Park. There were more players in the city than before and Horc wondered if that was just because more people had gotten off work and had logged on, or if there was something else going on. They all seemed to be in the first few levels of their characters, which if the beta had just opened up, made sense. Most of the players who saw him stared for a moment and gave him a wide berth.

Horc had no trouble finding Sureshot again. He nodded as Horc walked up.

"Ah, young Horc, you've returned. It looks like you've managed to kill the pigs I asked you to. If only the death of ten swine will make a real difference in our forest, but I suppose we all have to start somewhere." He reached into his bag and pulled out a dark green cloak. "Here is the reward I promised you."

Text appeared.

Quest: Swine Hunt Completed
Rewards 300 xp, Forest cloak, 25 copper
Reputation with Humans +10
Reputation with Rangers +50

Horc accepted the cloak, and the small bag of coins. "Thank you."

Sureshot grinned. "No, thank you, Horc. You have made our forest safer and dealt a blow to the efforts of the Gnoll king."

Horc taped his avatar icon and looked at his XP bar. It was over halfway to third level.

"Is there anything else I can do for you?" Horc asked.

"One of your brother Rangers is in the mountains to the south of here. He is working on rooting out the infestation of Gnolls. He could use every helping hand he can get." As soon as Sureshot finished his pitch, a quest box appeared.

Quest: Find Boris Brightbow
Rewards: 250 XP
Accept–Decline

"Accept."

"May the winds be kind to you on your quest." Sureshot knelt next to his wolf and rubbed its head. "The mountains can be a very dangerous place."

Horc glanced around at the other people standing in the grove. They were all NPCs. He looked at the text above each one of them. One was a Druid trainer, and two were merchants. One even said Bower.

He hurried over to the Bower. "Do you have arrows?"

The Bower bowed slightly. "But of course. What kind of arrows are you looking for, young ranger." He seemed to study Horc for a moment. "At your level, I only have basic arrows for you to use."

"Sure, how much?" Horc dug out the coin purse Sureshot had given him. He wished there were more coins in it.

"Twenty-five coppers for one hundred arrows."

It would take most of Horc's money. Then an idea hit him "Can I also turn in some of the loot I got off the pig here?"

"Of course," the Bower said. "Any merchant in town will be more than happy to buy from an outstanding citizen such as yourself."

Horc began emptying his bag onto the counter. The merchant sorted things into a couple of different piles. When he was done, he did a quick count of things. "Not much here, but I can give you ten copper for the measly loot you've returned from the forest with."

"Sounds decent. So how many arrows can I get for ten copper?"

"If you are also buying the one hundred arrows, I'll throw in another fifty for ten copper."

It didn't sound like a horrible deal. "I'll take them." At least he wasn't going to run out of arrows before he could complete the next quests. Horc's coin purse magically grew lighter and the arrows appeared in his empty quiver. "Thanks."

Feeling like he was ready to take on almost anything, Horc headed out of Druid Park and toward the main city gate.

Mike, how are you coming with your quest? Horc asked after he pulled up the chat window.

Mike's not here right now, it's just Baladara. Baladara replied.

Horc rolled his eyes. *Fine. Are you heading toward the gate with a new quest?*

Going to find a Mage in the mountains. I bet this starts a major quest chain.

Horc glanced at the map and Baladara's dot was approaching the gate faster than he was. The increased number of players made getting through the streets harder. He almost wished he wasn't using his pod and was more digital than physical. It would've been a lot easier to just walk through toons, but he couldn't. He had to dodge around them. *I'll be at the gate in a couple of minutes.*

No problem. I'm going to be AFK for a minute or two until you get here.

Horc continued making his way through the crowd, suddenly realizing that the bonus from corporate to beta test probably had everyone and their dog playing. He couldn't believe he hadn't heard any office chit-chat about the game until Mike had asked him, but he'd been busy since their morning briefing. He wasn't even sure he'd stopped for lunch. The odds were that the game was going to be packed every day during beta testing, which was probably a good thing, as it would help give the designers a better feel for how things would run and what the server capacity would be.

He neared the gates and spotted Baladara standing there. Her chin was resting on her chest and her eyes were closed. It looked like she was sleeping standing up. After a minute or so she jerked.

"Alan, you're at home in your pod, right?" Baladara looked frantic. "You're not in one of the public pod stores?"

"Right. What's wrong?"

"Dude, a tornado just wiped your neighborhood off the map."

Horc felt light headed. "What? How am I still here if my house was destroyed?" He pulled up the main game menu and stared at the buttons there. His Exit Game button was grayed out. He had no way to get out of the game. He was trapped.

5

"I CAN'T log out. Damn it Mike, I can't log out!" Alan wanted out of the game right then. He wanted to hit something, but other than the stone wall behind Baladara there wasn't anything unless he started assaulting players, and he didn't thing that would go over well. But he didn't like being trapped. He'd always been able to log out of a game whenever he wanted. He had no idea what was going on with his body and he was stuck in the game and in the pod.

"Don't freak out, dude, we'll figure this out." Baladara tapped the air in front of her.

"How? How are we going to figure anything out? I'm stuck in the damn game." Horc paced away from the gate, walking in a big circle as he continued to punch and swipe the grayed-out button that should send him back to his body.

"The pod… does it have a backup power battery?" Baladara asked.

"Sure. What's the point of having a pod if you don't have a backup power supply? But that doesn't explain why I'm stuck in the game." He'd never even encountered someone stuck in a game at work on a call with a frantic customer. There was no documentation on it, at least not to his knowledge. He wasn't used to not knowing what to do, and he didn't like the feeling.

"But it does explain why you're still in game even if your house has been destroyed. Is your pod above ground and in a basement?"

"What does that have to do with it? If the house is gone, the pod should be gone too." Horc didn't like the way he was on the verge of hysterics, but he had no idea why he was still alive if his house had collapsed and his pod had been crushed. He should already be dead.

"Dude, we do tech support for these pods," Baladara said. "What's one of the biggest selling points of our pods?"

"They're almost indestructible," Horc mumbled. Then he perked up. "Wait a minute, they're nigh indestructible. Mine's got the titanium shell. I figured if anything ever happened to the house, I might salvage the pod. I never expected to be in it when disaster struck." The switch over to back up power explained the flicker earlier, but he had no idea how long he could hold out, even with the pod doing its part to keep him alive.

"Right," Baladara agreed. "Even the cheaper models are reinforced construction. We've told people for a couple of years now that we could drop a house on one and it'd survive. It sounds like that's exactly what happened."

"I don't think we've ever told anyone they could survive a disaster in their pods, though." Horc came to a stop and stared at Baladara.

"Then you'll have a real-life story to add for the sales guys to help sell these things. I bet yours is still under warranty too. You'll get it replaced for nothing if it's got any damage."

"You're not helping." Horc started pacing again. The pacing helped push back some of the panic. He was stuck in his pod and would probably die there if nobody could get to his body before the power in the pod's backup battery ran out.

"Okay. I've got Lisa, the wife, on the phone now calling 911 so they'll know where to look for you. She's on hold, but someone will pick up eventually."

"And what are we supposed to do until then? Should I text my family and tell them I'm stuck in my pod, buried under the rubble of my house?" He knew his mother would completely freak out, but if she was watching the news and saw that his development had been destroyed, she was probably freaking out already.

Baladara shook her head. "I guess we can keep playing. See if we can put a few levels on these new toons. Lisa will understand if I stay in game with you until either the rescuers get to you, or I pass out from exhaustion."

Horc glared at her. "Keep playing. My pod… my body is trapped under the rubble of my house and you think I should keep playing?"

"Sure." Baladara put her hands on her hips and returned the glare. "Why not? It's not like there's anything else you can do until we can figure out why you can't log out. Even though the pod still has enough power to keep you in the game, if something was massively wrong with the pod, you'd be back there. Alan, stop and think about this for a moment. How would you react to waking up in a steel and plexi-coffin with no light and a bunch of crap on top of you? Dude, it would be like being buried alive. At least here you've got things you can do and keep your mind occupied until we get the problems worked out."

It made a lot more sense than Horc wanted to admit. If there was debris on top of the pod, there would be no way for him to get out. He didn't want to holler himself hoarse hoping someone would hear him and come rescue him. At least if they had a way to use Lisa as a mouthpiece between him and the rescue parties, they'd know he was still alive. He hated the idea that he was just going to keep playing a damned game while people tried to find him, but there wasn't much more he could do and just standing around waiting for something to happen would drive him nuts.

Horc let out a heavy sigh. "Alright. We'll play this your way. But Lisa better keep us informed of what's going on."

Baladara grinned and nodded. "Not a problem. Remember, I'm VR and not pod. She'll let me know every time she learns anything new or interesting. If I suddenly stop during a fight, make sure I don't die."

"Okay." Horc stopped pacing and looked at the gate out of the city. There was a lot worse situations he could be in. He might as well make the most of it and earn his beta testing bonus. He just hoped he didn't die before someone found his pod and dug him out.

6

A FEW minutes after clearing the main gate of Stone Helm City, Horc had to admit that being out and doing something was a lot easier than sitting around waiting for something to happen. He couldn't stop from wondering what was going on in the real world while he was gaming, but the warm evening breeze that carried the scent of fresh-cut grass and distant smoke helped him get lost in the illusion of being safe.

With Baladara at his side, Horc passed the spot in the road where they'd turned before to go on the pig hunt. The road dipped down a long hill and out across a pristine valley. There were a few small houses and farmsteads spread out across the valley. Here and there, cows grazed. If it hadn't just been a game, it would've been an ideal place to settle down for a long happy life.

"They really did a good job with this," Baladara said. "I wonder how long they've been working on the game. I mean, if we're beta testing and they're this far along, I'm going to bet for years."

"Probably as long as they worked on developing the pods," Horc said. "Maybe longer. Maybe they came up with the idea for the game, then decided they needed the pods to go with it."

"Sometimes the delivery system is born from the invention," Baladara replied.

A bolt of energy came from their left and hit Horc hard enough to send him staggering off the road.

"What the hell?" Horc regained his balance and stared up the hill where three players were rushing toward them.

"Die ye filthy Orc scum!" one shouted.

"Hey! Wait a minute." Baladara jumped between them and Horc. "What are you idiots doing?"

"That piece of dung doesn't belong amongst good light-fearing folk." The speaker stopped and began moving his hands to work another spell.

Baladara slapped his hands and the glow stopped. "Really? This beta has been going on for what, an hour? And you're already trying to kill other characters?" Baladara stopped and stared at the player as his friends had stopped behind him and had the decency to look confused. "Wait…Stan? Stan from the mail room?"

The player, puffed out his chest. "I don't know who you're talking about. I am Lord Stanis Holy Smite." He pulled a huge hammer from his belt. "Now stand down or face my wrath."

The blue text above the player did say **Stanishollyshmite, Human, Paladin, Level 2**.

"You are Stan." Baladara put her hands on her hips. "Only Stan Smith from the mailroom gets this into character. Stan, stop it. You're acting like an idiot."

Stan looked confused. "And whom be you?"

Baldara nodded so hard she rocked back and forth. "Yep, definitely Stan. Nobody else would even think about saying 'whom.' Stan, did you even stop to read the what passes for a wiki right now or look at the characters or races we can play? No, you probably didn't. You always run a pally, always human. Stan, if you don't want me to make your life hell at work for the next few months, back down now."

"But you travel with an Orc." Stanis looked from Baladara to Horc. "Orcs are foul creatures."

"Half-Orc, Stan." Horc walked over and stood next to Baladara, wishing he had his blaster and not just a sword. At least with a blaster, he could put it on stun and knock the fool out. And if she was right and this was Stan from the mailroom, it might be nice to render him unconscious a few times. "That means I start out neutral between light and dark. It doesn't give you the right to attack me just because you want to be an ass."

"He's right, Stanis," his friend, **Lefthandofgod, Human, Paladin, level 2** said. "Look at his alignment bar. He's neutral heading toward light. If we kill him, we'll lose prestige and we don't want that."

The other player, **Righthandofgod, Human, Paladin, level 2** stayed quiet.

Stanis stared at Horc. "Okay, who are you two, IRL? How do you know who I am?"

Baladara, with her hands still on her hips frowned at him. "I'm Mike Simmons from tech support. This is Alan Gosling, you know, our lead, one step away from being a manager. You just attacked someone in *management*."

Instantly, Stanis' demeanor changed. "Ah man, Mr. Gosling. I *am* so sorry. I had no idea. I was just getting into character. You know how it is."

Horc nodded. "I know how it is. Just please, don't do it again."

"I promise, I won't go after you again." Stanis bowed low. "We're cool, right?"

"Cool." Horc understood it was just a game and he wasn't going to push things with Stan. Odds were if he managed to survive and get out of the game, he'd never bring up the incident, if Stan didn't.

"Thanks. Okay. We've got some Paladin quests to finish up. Have fun." Stanis turned and hurried back the way they'd come, with his two friends following silently along behind him.

"Man, sometimes I really worry about Stan and his kind of nerds," Baladara said. "You'd think they don't have much of a life outside of gaming."

"Gaming and work." Horc nodded as they continued down the road. "I can understand. I probably put a little too much time into my preferred game. I also put in a little too much time in the daily grind too. Maybe I need to find more to my life."

"Don't let Lisa know I said this, but sometimes I think folks make a little too much out of the whole home and family thing," Baladara said. "There's plusses to it, but I think I'd like to try the single guy mode for a while and just see what it's like."

"I won't tell her," Horc promised. He'd never met Mike's wife, but Mike didn't normally have anything bad to say about her. Although if she cut into his gaming time, he could understand.

A figure shimmered into existence and stood in the middle of the road before them. It was a tall young woman in long gray robes. Her brown hair was cut into a short bob, and she carried a staff.

"Horc the Ranger?" the woman asked, looking between Horc and Baladara.

There wasn't any text above her head, and that made Horc nervous.

Slowly easing his hand toward the pommel of his sword, Horc responded, "Yeah. Please tell me you're not here to challenge me for being a Half-Orc in Human lands."

"No, no. I'm Miranda from game support, one of the admins. We've gotten the messages Baladara sent both about the bug earlier and about your pod being damaged in a tornado with you in it. How are you feeling?"

Horc eased his hand away from his sword and frowned. "Feeling? As in physically or emotionally? Physically, I guess I'm fine. Pain hurts, water tastes great, my feet are a little sore from all the walking. Emotionally, I'm trying to be okay, but I'm terrified that I'm never going to get out of that pod."

Miranda nodded and leaned on her staff. "Okay. That's all totally understandable. We're trying to see what's going on with your interface. We've never seen anything like it before. Theoretically, if the pods are damaged, you should be logged out of whatever game you're playing at the time and returned to the pod. Since that hasn't happened, we're assuming the best, that being that your pod wasn't damaged in the tornado. We've sent a pod recovery team to your house, but unfortunately all the roads for about twenty miles have been blocked by the storm."

Horc's head swam. "Wait a minute. Twenty miles? How big was the storm? How long was it on the ground?"

"It was one of the newer EF7s. Biggest ever recorded in Texas. The only tornado bigger, on record was an EF8 that leveled Kansas City to the bedrock last year." She shook her head and leaned on her staff. "Climate change is making it next to impossible to predict these things anymore, and everything's just getting worse. But that doesn't help you right now."

Horc sat down in the road and stared at her. He'd heard the news about the storm in Kansas City. It had killed hundreds of thousands of people. The cleanup effort had taken months. His house had just been in the middle of another such storm. How long would it take for the rescuers to reach him? Would the pod keep him alive that long? Sure, he'd gotten the deluxe model with every bell and whistle available, but he'd never counted on having a house fall on it, and him. Although he and Mike were part of the tech support team for the pods, he didn't know all their details. They both knew how to look up things using Google, but that was about it.

"I'm going to die in here, aren't I?" Horc mumbled.

Miranda shook her head and squatted down in front of him. "Not if I can help it. We're all going to be working around the clock to get you out of here. From this end, we're trying to determine what happened and why you don't have an option to exit the game. That's one of the fail-safe protocols that shouldn't have malfunctioned. Everyone should be able to log out whenever they want…well, as long as they aren't in battle—that would be cheating. We've contacted the original programmer team and they're all en route to the main server site in Austin."

"That's good, but logging out won't do me any good until the pod's recovered, right?" Horc rubbed his face. He'd thought he was dealing with everything fairly well, but Miranda wasn't helping him in the least.

"Right. But I'll let you know as soon as your pod's out of the rubble and connected to power again."

Horc nodded. Then something hit him. "Will we be able to tell here in game if my body is dying in the real world?"

"We can't know for sure. Again, this is all theoretical, but you should start to feel weak and disoriented here in game if your body is dying IRL."

"Okay. Do me a favor. We know where I am. Don't make my retrieval a priority at this time. There's got to be a ton of other people trapped or dead. Save other people first. Tell the retrieval team to not pass by others to get to me. I'm just a lowly middle management guy in corporate America. Right now, I'm safe in my pod. I should be okay, for a couple of days, if it performs as advertised."

Miranda pursed her lips and stood. "Alan, that's very brave of you. I'll pass that along. One word of warning. You might want to do what you can to stay alive in game.

Since your interface is malfunctioning, we don't know what will happen if you die in here."

"Wait--What?" One of the fun things about all games was not having to worry about staying alive. Even games like Halfworld brought the characters back to life, there might be some struggle to get back to where you left off, but death wasn't really dead, just inconvenient.

"Miranda, if you haven't noticed, we're both second level," a level of panic tinged Baladara's voice. "Most of the game can wipe us out without raising a sweat."

"I know." Miranda closed her eyes. "It would be better if Horc just goes back to town and sits around in an inn somewhere and drinks until we can recover the pod and safely log you out." She gripped her staff. "I'll find you again when I have more information to give you."

"Hold on a second." Horc stood so he was on eye level with her. "Town's not even safe. I've got players threatening me because I'm a Half-Orc."

She shrugged. "We designed the game to have challenges like that. There's nothing I can do to stop it. Although I'll talk to the designers and see if they can come up with something to help. But until either they come up with something, or we can get you out of the game, stay safe." She tapped her staff on the ground and vanished.

Horc turned to Baladara. "Well this's just a fine mess. It just keeps getting better and better. Why didn't you tell me it was an EF7 tornado that took out my neighborhood? Hell that large of a storm probably took out most of Garland."

"And part of Mesquite." Baladara said. "We got lucky it didn't take out Carrolton too. I didn't want you to worry. Dude, we're going to get you through this."

Horc huffed and started walking down the road as it leveled out into the valley. "Okay, I guess I can appreciate that. But I'm not going back to town. We're going to play this on the safe side and try to level up fast so I don't have to worry as much about dying in here. If I go back to town, I'll go bonkers in a few hours. Maybe Miranda and the developers can come up with something quickly."

"I'm right here for you." Baladara strolled alongside Horc. "I'll do everything I can to keep you alive. I promise."

Having a lot of people working toward his continued existence made Horc feel a little better. But he still knew it was just a matter of time before they encountered something they couldn't deal with, or before a player hell-bent on killing every Orc and Half-Orc in the game crossed their path and he was going to be in trouble.

7

HORC CHECKED his map. Even after crossing the green valley, they still had a fair distance to go before they reached their destination. A yellow dot just replaced the silver arrow on the far edge of his map. "We're getting closer."

"Yeah, but I bet this area is something the game designers are still trying to finish up," Baladara said. "It doesn't make sense to have this much dead space so close to a major town. Players won't like that."

"So what do you think they'll put here?" Horc thought everything looked fairly finished. The little farmsteads all had buildings, fences, and livestock. He couldn't really see where it could need more.

"The fast thing would to put quest starting points in here. You know, maybe one of the farmers is having trouble with wolves eating his sheep, or the pigs sent by the Gnoll King raiding the garden. But part of what I read about Halfworld was that people were going to be able to buy real estate as they got enough levels and gold to do so. Giving players a real stake in the game might make people play more." Baladara glanced around. "Yeah, I can definitely see them subdividing this area so players can have homes near the city. I bet that comes along in future expansions."

"But doesn't that mess with the whole medieval fantasy feel of the game when you start buying houses and such?" Horc liked the landscape he saw and the fairly peaceful feel to the whole thing. A subdivision, even if it was made up of thatched houses and not brick condos, didn't feel right. If that happened, Horc was fairly sure he'd stop playing as soon as the beta testing time was up and he got his bonus.

"Some games are going to that level of realism," Baladara said. "I mean, don't you have your own space ship in the other game?"

"Yeah, but that's different. That's a space ship, not a house like I can really buy." A cow wandered over to the fence and Horc rubbed its nose in passing. It was soft and velvety. He'd never touched a real cow and had no idea how close to authentic the feeling was, but was amazed that his pod and the game interface made it feel like he was touching a cow.

"I'm betting more than a few people will spend way too much time in this game and it'll become like a second home to them." Baladara kicked a rock down the road. It rolled a short distance and stopped, but the tumbling sound it made was very real. "In some cases this place might be a lot better than where they live IRL and they might not want to leave."

Horc ran his hand along the rough timber of the fence that kept the cows out of the road. "I've heard of people who have pods in efficiency apartments and they only leave them a couple hours a day, to keep their muscles from completely atrophying. I hope my life never becomes that bleak."

"Those people are the reason there's a rise in gamer drugs to keep people awake for days on end. With more games like Halfworld coming online all the time, I wouldn't be surprised if lawmakers don't start passing regulations to stop people from spending too much time in their pods, forcing them to get out and smell the real roses."

"The game corps will fight them tooth and nail," Horc said as the fence ended and they started up out of the valley. "And nowadays, they're almost as powerful as the tobacco and alcohol companies." As personal entertainment became a larger and larger industry, the big corporations that controlled what reached the public had decided that the drug, alcohol and tobacco companies had the right idea with having politicians under their thumbs. It was helping keep their industry from being over regulated.

Baladara nodded and kicked another stone. "Yeah, they did manage to stop video game regs back in the days when everyone was convinced that violent games were contributing to gun terrorism."

"So as long as they keep their fingers on their favorite officials, people will be able to abuse themselves with their games as much as they want."

Up the hill, a man sat scowling at the digital landscape.

Horc couldn't imagine what was causing the man to just sit there. He wore green robes and had a staff lying in front of him. When he focused on him, the text above him said. **Greensleeves, Human, Druid, level 2**. He was a player, which made Horc even more curious about why he was just sitting there.

"Hey, is everything okay?" Horc called out.

Greensleeves looked up. "I'm already fed up."

"With what?" Horc walked off the road and up the hill.

"This stupid game." Greensleeves made a sweeping gesture. "Honestly, if I didn't need the bonus, I wouldn't even be in here."

"Hey, it's not a rough game." Baladara leaned on her staff and peered at Greensleeves. "Fairly standard with easy quests."

"But most of the players are assholes." Greensleeves muttered.

"A few," Horc agreed. "But we're not assholes. What happened?"

Greensleeves huffed. "I was heading over to the mountains. Second level quest. Minding my own business when I got jumped by three players, all level five warriors. They killed me and took my loot. When I got back to my body, they were standing here and killed me again. They did that three times until I finally just logged out for a while. Went and had a beer. When I logged back on, they were gone, but I don't know if the bonus is going to be worth it if I can't have at least a little bit of fun."

Baladara straightened and stared at Greensleeves. "Wait a minute. How are they level fives? We just got access to the game this afternoon."

Horc had to agree, it had taken the two of them a little bit of time to get to level two, and he figured that each level would take longer to get through.

"I figure they're from one of the European offices, they got access to the game yesterday," Greensleeves said. "I'm betting from the way they were acting they're from either Dublin or Paris. Most of the other offices have more mature people on staff. Dublin has the youngest people in the company."

"Wow, I didn't know they'd opened the beta up to the whole company," Horc said. "Why aren't we seeing more players? Where are you from? We're out of the Dallas office."

"Atlanta." Greensleeves pushed himself up on his staff so he stood with them. "I bet a lot of people are playing other races. You two are the first non-humans I've seen. How did you start at Stone Helm City?"

"I got the choice," Horc said. "As a Half-Orc, I had the option of either going to the Human or Orc starting zone."

"I saw where Horc was, and we wanted to run together, so I asked a guard in Eledorra to get me here," Baladara said. "It was a long shot, but it worked."

Greensleeves shook his head. "That shouldn't have worked. My husband's one of the designers and he explained everything to me before I logged on. That's why I went with Human. I normally run Elves, but he wanted me to try out some of the dungeons in this area first. Said they were more interesting than the dungeons in the Elf starting zone. If I'd known we could just ask guards to get us to another city, I would've done that."

"Wait," Horc said. "Your husband's a designer. Is he working on my problem?"

"What problem is that?" Greensleeves asked. "Right now all the senior designers are working on some guy in Texas."

Horc nodded. "That's me. My house got destroyed in a tornado. I was in my pod at the time. Now I can't log out, and we don't know what's happening"

"That's the one. He told me a little while I was drinking my beer. Dude, that's rough. Rick's trying to make sure if something happens to you in game, that you're going to be alright." Greensleeves got an excited look in his eyes. "Hey, are you two up for another party member? I'm going to take the healer track when we get that far along. Right now I have simple healer spells. I could help keep you alive."

Horc didn't mind someone else running with them as long as they were decent. He glanced at Baladara.

She nodded. "Sure, let's run together. We've got to do what we can to keep Alan…I mean Horc, alive."

Greensleeves offered Horc his hand. "I'm David IRL. Thanks for letting me run with you two. We can help keep each other alive…well as long as we don't have a party of high-level assholes hit us."

"Thanks, David…Greensleeves." Horc said, then Greensleeves's icon appeared below Baladara's on the left side of Horc's screen. "Okay, did he just join the party by our handshake?"

Baladara laughed. "You really are a newb with this game. No. I sent him a party invite." She took Greensleeves's hand. "I'm Mike IRL. Horc normally doesn't play fantasy games. He's more of a sci-fi gamer."

"Really?" Greensleeves asked. "Which game? I actually prefer those too. I think they're more stimulating and can see them expanding our future."

"Galactic Explorers." Horc said.

"Me too. What's your toon's name?"

"Captain Malfoy."

"Of the starship Finder. I've heard of you." Greensleeves sounded excited. "We'll have to try to connect in there too, once we get you out of your pod, that is."

Horc nodded. "Yeah. Once I get out, I might not want to get back in for a while."

"I hear you there. That must be scary. I think I'd just go sit in one of the inns and drink mead until they rescued me."

Horc decided they could walk while they talked. He gestured for them to head up the hill. "I'd go nuts doing that. Might as well try to have some fun."

"I understand that too," Greensleeves said. "Tell you what, if we follow the quest chains we're currently on, we should all end up in the same place, which is going to take us into a fantastic dungeon. Rick's really proud of it 'cause he was one of the main designers of the Human zone."

"If he's one of the designers, could you please explain why there's so little close to town?" Baladara asked. "Unless we just want to grind on pigs, there's not much to get started with."

"From my understanding, the thought behind not having much around the main cities was twofold," Greensleeves said as they walked up the hill. "First, it's to help push players out to explore more quickly. Second, it's for future expansion. They've already got plans for the first expansion of the game. It should be out about six months after they go live. The goal is to keep things changing and new to hold players' attention."

"Makes sense, but still it makes things a little boring to start with," Baladara said. "Even if the level of realism is higher than any game I've played before. I'm still on VR and it's blowing me away."

"It's even better via pod." Greensleeves rubbed his side. "I'm still hurting from where those assholes killed me."

Horc wasn't sure if he wanted to know how much it hurt to die in the game. Although he hadn't checked, he wouldn't be surprised if the pig that had been several levels above them hadn't left bruises in its attack. Although his health was full, Horc still thought he could feel a tinge from that spot from time to time as he hiked along, but that was likely either just his imagination or another malfunction. It was beginning to seem like his entire time in game was one malfunction after another.

8

WHEN THEY reached the top of the hill, they were looking into another valley, but there was a lot more activity in this one. A small camp occupied the center of the valley, and players were running among the tents. Most of the players disappeared into the forest on either side of the camp. There were a few who ran into camp, and then took off down the road, continuing away from Stone Helm City.

"Okay, this is more like what I was expecting," Baladara said. "I guess we're just moving too slow… the drawbacks of traveling with a newb."

"A newb who's in a major mess right now," Horc said, although he smiled since he knew Baladara was giving him grief in a lame attempt to get him to relax and not worry about his situation out of game.

"I was expecting something more like this too," Greensleeves confessed. "Let's get down there and turn these quests in so we can get the next link in the chains."

They seemed to be the only characters who were walking and not running. "So, are we the lame ones too?" Horc asked. "Everyone else is running."

"And most likely wearing their stamina down," Greensleeves said. "There's a huge benefit to not running everywhere. You don't run out of energy as fast. We might not finish as many quests as quickly, but we'll do more damage and last in fights longer. We're okay."

"That must be a new feature," Baladara said. "I've never run into that in a game before."

"Trying to incorporate more of the benefits of the pods," Greensleeves said. "From what Rick says, they're trying to figure out more real world uses for the pods beyond just gaming. If paraplegics can use the pods to help them exercise and improve their health, that's a good thing. It might also help with long-distance space travel."

"Also helps the company make more money," Horc said. "Come on, if there wasn't money in it, the company wouldn't be worried about it."

"Yeah, that's true." Greensleeves said as they reached the flat spot in the valley. "So do we stay together, or drop off our quests and get back together after we receive our new ones?"

"We can just follow the dots on the map," Horc said. "It'll be faster to split up."

"Faster, now you're talking." Baladara grinned and then bounced off.

"He knows how to work that Elf, doesn't he?" Greensleeves said. "Do you know him IRL?"

Following the arrow toward the edge of the tents, Horc nodded. "Yeah. He surprised me with the female Elf. I never would've expected it of him. I can't figure out the guys who play girls in game."

"Some say they like looking at female bodies more than male, but that's when they're using VR and not the pods." Greensleeves continued to walk next to him. "I haven't run into that with podpeople. They tend to want to look like improved versions of themselves."

"I can see that. Don't think I'm just a big green-skinned guy IRL." Horc chuckled. "I just used random on nearly everything the system would let me. But I wasn't going to be a girl."

"I'll keep that in mind." Greensleeves said. "I think our turn-ins are next to each other."

Horc saw the Ranger he was looking for and next to him stood a Druid. "Looks that way."

Boris Brightbow, the imposing Ranger Horc was supposed to find, had a huge black bear standing next to him. He grinned as Horc approached. He reached out a large hand to Horc. "Greetings Horc. It is good that Caleb Sureshot could send me help. The situation here in the Azurcliff Mountains is dire. The Gnoll king and his minions are advancing their attack on our people."

"Anything I can do to help."

Quest: Find Boris Brightbow Completed
Reward: 250 XP
Reputation with Humans +10
Reputation with Druids +30

Horc checked his XP bar and it was nearly three quarters of the way to third level. He hoped it wouldn't take too many kills to level.

"There's lots you can do to help," Brightbow said. "We believe the Gnoll king and his minions are disturbing the natural wildlife in the area. Over recent weeks, the wolves have become particularly aggressive. We need them thinned out."

After a second a window popped up.

Quest: Clear the way
Objective: Kill fifteen wolves.
Rewards: 300 XP
25 copper
Bow of the Wolf Slayer
Accept—Reject

Horc said "Accept.".

"Many thanks, Horc. Be wary—some of the wolves can be very dangerous."

"I'll do my best." Horc turned and noticed that the Druid who Greensleeves was talking to had the yellow glow of a quest giver.

"Hey, can we get more than one quest at a time?"

"Sure." Greensleeves turned and looked like he was about finished with the Druid. "You can have up to fifty quests at one time. Although if you ask me, that gets rather burdensome after a while. It also ends up with crossing quest chains and losing max XP you can get from them if you level too fast for the quests."

"Okay, this just keeps getting more complicated." Horc rubbed his head. "Should I take his quest or not?"

"Probably. If it's the same one I just took, it's for wolf skins." Greensleeves looked past Horc at Brightbow. "Is his for killing wolves?"

"Yeah."

"Then the two quests are part of the same chain. Taking both will save you time." Greensleeves walked past Horc. "Just talk to him and see."

Horc approached **Verdant Longstaff, Human, Druid, level 20**. Verdant Longstaff looked older than most of the NPCs Horc had seen, even had gray hair and hands that looked like they were swollen with arthritis.

"Hi, how can I help you?" Horc asked. He was still figuring out the best way to get the NPCs to give him quests. He knew in some games, players had to ask the right questions to get the correct responses.

"Blessings young Ranger," Verdant replied. "These hills are a very dangerous place, but also very cold in the winter and we are anticipating a long campaign against the Gnoll king. If you could bring me 10 wolf pelts, I would be greatly appreciative. I would make it worth your while."

A window appeared.

Quest: Skins for the winter
Objective: Bring Verdant Longstaff 10 wolf pelts
Rewards: 300 XP
25 copper
Heavy Wolf Pelt Clock Armor 8
Accept--Reject

Horc accepted the quest.

Verdant bowed. "Thank you, young Ranger. By thinning out the wolves that have overrun these hills, we'll make it easier for them to survive the winter."

"I'll do my best." Horc returned the bow and looked at Greensleeves. "I wonder if Baladara's Mage trainer also has a quest we can get."

"Not sure about that one, but there are a few more over there." Greensleeves pointed to a couple other NPCs standing in front of the next cluster of tents.

"Okay." Horc didn't want to get too many quests, but wanted to grab what was available to make the most of his time and level quickly. The higher level he was, the less likely he was to run into trouble with other players who were out to be bullies in the cyber fantasy world.

A few minutes later, the three of them had gotten all the quests available and joined the other players rushing out into the forest around them.

"So how should we do this?" Horc asked.

"Let's head deeper into the zone," Baladara suggested. "With all the players around, it'll take more time for the mobs to respawn and we'll have to be right on top of things if we hope to kill things and get XP."

"Sounds good," Greensleeves said with a nod. "I'm going to assume you both have enough food and drink to keep you going."

"Yeah, we're good." Baladara patted the pouch on her hip.

Horc had a few things but hoped he didn't end up needing much—only time would tell.

"Then let's do this." Greensleeves bounced his staff against his palm and stalked off into the forest that showed a soft red glow on Horc's map.

The first wolf appeared from behind a tree when they'd taken about five steps into the area. It was a big fierce-looking beast, but its text said it was only level 3.

It was a Mountain Wolf. They all unleashed their assaults at the same time. Horc's arrow hit the wolf first. Red text rolled up, showing 25 damage. As the wolf howled and rushed him, Baladara and Greensleeves' magic hit at the same time for a total of another forty damage. The combined damage dropped the wolf to nearly half. Without a word, they all hit it again. Horc fired a third arrow before the others had time to get their spells off. The wolf slid to a stop and collapsed at their feet.

40 XP rolled through Horc's vision. He knelt next to the wolf and collected his loot. He got a bit of wolf meat, but nothing else.

"Okay, I got a pelt," Baladara said, "but no gallbladder."

"I got the gallbladder," Greensleeves said.

"I wonder if this means we can't all get the same quest items from the same kill," Horc said.

Baladara shrugged. "Hard to say. Things like that vary from game to game. Since this is a beta, we don't know for sure until we have a few more kills under our belt." She stared at Greensleeves. "Unless someone's husband has given them a clue on some things, beyond the Human dungeon being more interesting than the Elf one."

Greensleeves laughed as he slipped the gallbladder into his bag. "Nope. He's given me a few hints, but nothing like that. We can write an article in the wiki if we want, once we figure out how things work."

"Then let's keep going," Horc said. "We can kill thirty or forty of these things if we need to." He glanced around. "Not a ton of players this far out. I guess that makes it easier for us."

"Definitely." Baladara grinned and shot a spell over Horc's shoulder.

Horc jumped. "Damn it, warn a guy." He pulled an arrow and sighted the wolf that was charging them.

Again, it took three shots to bring the creature down. When they all got their loot, Horc ended up with the pelt. Over the next few wolves, they decided they weren't going to see multiple drops of quest items and settled in for a long round of farming the items they needed. But at least the wolves were getting them all XP, and would help the three of them gain levels.

9

"OKAY, WHAT do I do? I'm out of bag space," Horc mumbled as he got down to just needing one more pelt. A fair number of the things the wolves had dropped stacked in his bags, like the pelts, but more things didn't, like random pieces of armor, and an axe. The armor and the axe looked like they'd been chewed on, but when he studied them, they showed a value, all in coppers, but nothing in silver or gold. He hadn't really expected anything major from wolves that were quickly becoming lower level than he was.

Baladara screwed up her face and stared at him. "What do you mean you're out of bag space? Didn't you buy extra bags?"

A wave of stupidity rolled over Horc. "Buy extra bags? Can we put bags inside of bags?"

Greensleeves finished looting the latest wolf and shook his head. "No, but you can buy extra bags. Your initial bag only has twenty-five slots. That fills up really fast if you're having to grind on mobs like we're doing right now. I still need one more gallbladder."

"Two pelts here," Baladara said after a quick check of her bag.

"One more pelt for me," Horc said. "But what do I do if I end up getting something that won't go into a stack, or is more than my stacks will hold?"

"Then we juggle things between us until we get back to town so we can hit the bag vendor. We've made enough for you to be able to get at least a small bag, maybe two." Baladara sighed and scanned the forest. "I can't believe you didn't think to get more bag space after the first couple of quests."

"We don't worry about bag space where I normally play," Horc said. "This kind of questing thing is new to me."

"Don't worry about it." Greensleeves started walking through the forest. "I've got plenty of storage if we need it. I don't want Rick helping out too much, although he offered, but I did let him max out my bags once I had the toon up and running."

Baladara whistled. "Maxed your bag space out? That's awesome. You can never have too many spots in your bags."

"I totally agree," Greensleeves said. "Why do you think I let my husband give me a little cheat like that?"

"So how do I get things to you?" Horc asked. He supposed he could just pull things out of his bag and lay them on the ground.

"If you want, we can clear out the non-quest items now," Greensleeves offered.

"Sure."

Greensleeves tapped in the air and a box appeared between them. Across the top it said trade window. "This is faster than taking things out of your bags and physically…or is that digitally…give them to me."

There were five spaces on the trade window and Horc opened up the window that displayed everything he had in his bags. He quickly moved five items, things that wouldn't stack, over.

A quizzical look crossed Greensleeves' face. "Are you sure you can't use any of these?"

"Use them? You mean replace what I've got on with this stuff?" It was something else that hadn't crossed Horc's mind. He figured he was going to have to buy new armor and weapons every so often. He hadn't considered that better stuff might be just lying around in the loot from monsters he killed.

"Sure," Baladara said. "Look, let's take a minute and see if any of this stuff is better than what you've got, or if any of us have things the others can use."

"Okay." It wasn't like they were in any sort of hurry to finish up gaming and log off for the night. "What's the best way to do that?"

"We're all partied together, so we can see each other's stuff through the party chat window." Baladara was frantically tapping the air in front of her.

Horc moved his hands to expand his chat window to something larger so he could see everything. Character sheets popped up as did everyone's bags. They all had more gear than Horc had expected. There was an assortment of things, swords, axes, armor of various makes.

"Okay, so we haven't gotten anything really awesome yet," Baladara said. "None of us can use chain or plate armor at this point so all that shit gets sold. Horc, as a Ranger, you can use the axe, let's see if it's better than what you have."

Horc looked at his character sheet and tapped the spot where his sword was. It said.

Apprentice short sword
One handed
Damage 1-3
Speed 2

He looked at the axe currently residing in Greensleeves bag among the other items he'd passed over to him for holding.

Axe of the Wolf Slayer
One handed
Damage 5-8
Speed 3

"Okay, so it looks like the axe is better than what I have."

"Let me give that back to you," Greensleeves said, and a trade window opened up between them. The axe was in it.

Horc tapped on the trade button and the axe was back in his bag. He pulled the axe out and looked at it. The leather on the handle was in rough shape with numerous bite marks, but the blade itself was shiny and looked to have a nice edge. He put the sword in the bag where the axe had been, and hung the axe from his belt.

"Hey, I think this robe is an improvement over what I have," Baladara said. She turned her back to them and quickly changed. The new robe was a bright purple with stars around the hem and cuffs. "Yeah, definitely."

"Okay, so now that we're done exchanging stuff out, let's get back to wolf slaying." Greensleeves turned and strolled deeper into the forest. "Horc, when we get back to the encampment, let's see if there's a vendor there you can buy bags from. Out here in the wild, it might not be as cheap as they would be either from a specialty bag vendor, another player, or the flea market."

"Wait a minute, this place has a flea market?" Horc shook his head. It was a bit hard for him to believe that.

"Yeah, but since we're in the first day of beta testing, it's probably not as well stocked as it will be in a couple of months when the game goes live." Greensleeves paused and pointed. It was their agreed upon signal that there was a target ahead.

"I guess it's just another term for the auction house I'm used to in Galactic Explorers," Horc said as he pulled out his bow and strung an arrow. He couldn't see anything, but he trusted Greensleeves.

"Yeah, a lot of these games all have the same basic setup and ideas. They just use different names for things." Greensleeves began casting his spell. His hands moved and glowed green. "Rick's fairly proud of the flea market. He and his team worked hard on it and I'm supposed to start selling things in there as soon as I can." He finished his spell and a bolt of green light shot from his hands as Horc stepped far enough to his side to see the wolf.

Horc released his arrow. It hit the wolf hard, knocking on its side. Baladara's spell hit seconds later and the thing went down.

25XP flashed on the screen.

A golden aura surrounded Horc and bold gold text scrolled down his vision.

Level 5.

A series of messages flashed.

Talent tree now open
Training now available
Professions now available

"Yay, you hit level 5!" Baladara cheered. "I think I've only got another couple of kills before I hit that."

"Me too," Greensleeves said.

Horc checked the carcass for loot. There was his final wolf pelt. Also a couple of copper to be split between him and the others.

His screen flashed.

Quest: Skins for the winter complete.

"I'm done with this quest," Horc said. "Now let's hope your drops will be faster."

Baladara laughed. "You're calling the loot drops. We'll make a fantasy gamer out of you yet."

Horc frowned. "We call them drops in sci-fi games too."

There was a roar and a huge bear came charging out of the forest. Horc's window flashed red as the bear came right at him.

"Hit it!" Baladara shouted as her hands began to move to cast a spell.

Lighting lanced out of the sky. It was one of Greensleeve's instacast spells. It hit the bear but it continued rushing toward Horc. As Horc targeted the bear red text appeared above its head. **Forest Grizzly level 7**.

"Guys, it's a level seven!" Horc swung his new axe and managed a glancing blow.

The words **One Handed Axe Skill 2** appeared on his screen.

He wondered why he hadn't seeing that with either his bow or his short sword but wrote it off to them being apprentice weapons. Baladara's spell hit the bear, and its health bar dropped, but there was still plenty of fight left in it. Horc wished he could fall back and do damage from a distance. As a party they'd gotten coordinated so that most of the wolves hadn't gotten close enough to do damage to any of them, but the bear had taken them by surprise.

The bear hit Horc again, and his own health bar flared. It was still green, but had dropped enough he could see the damage piling up. Not to mention, it hurt.

With a battle roar almost as loud as the bear, Horc smashed the axe down on its furry head as hard as he could.

The bear's health dropped to nearly half, then a ball of green light hit it, followed by Baladara's blue magical bolt of power. The bear took more damage. But still had plenty of health. Trying to ignore the pain in his leg from where the bear had caught him good, Horc swung the axe again. It caught the bear in the eye. At the same time, Greensleeves caught it with another bolt of lightning. The bear's health bar flashed orange.

Horc swung hard again, catching the thing in the head. Baladara's magic bolt caught it from the other side. The bear staggered. Horc hit it again. The bear went down hard.

"It's down!" Horc cheered, then wobbled. He felt weak. His own health bar was flashing red and continuing to fall.

"Hold on!" Greensleeves shouted and rushed to Horc's side. "Let me get you healed."

"Okay." Remembering Miranda's warning, Horc really didn't want to die. The bear's attack had been the first time he'd taken major damage. Running with friends was helping to keep him safe.

Greensleeves moved his hands and chanted something in a strange language. A soft blue glow radiated out from him and encompassed Horc. His health bar shot up to half and stopped blinking red.

"Let me do that one more time." Greensleeves said and started his spell.

"Don't you two need to worry about mana?" Horc said, thankful his head wasn't spinning anymore and his health bar was rapidly going to where it needed to be.

"You must've missed the light show," Baladara said. "When the bear went down, we both leveled. We're all fifth level now. We topped off with leveling" She bent over the bear and set to looting the carcass.

"Cool." Horc said as Greensleeves finished his healing spell and his health bar returned to max. His coin purse clinked as ten coppers appeared.

Greensleeves dusted his hands off. "Okay, we don't need to fight things two levels above us very often, at least not until we improve our weapons and spells. I don't know about you two, but I need to head back to town for training, once we finish this quest."

Baladara nodded. "Definitely. Just need a couple more items. Can't we check the encampment for trainers?"

"Nope." Greensleeves shook his head. "Rick says the designers are working on getting more trainers programed, but right now they are just in the major cities.

I think one of the things they're going ask us is where we'd like to see both class trainers and profession trainers."

"All over the damned place," Baladara said. "If we need training, I don't want to have to go hiking all the way back to town, particularly when we're in the middle of a quest chain like this."

"I hear you," Greensleeves agreed. "Now, let's get these last few wolves."

As they resumed their trek through the forest, Horc was a lot more cautious. He'd come close to dying and none of them knew if that was going to be a very bad thing. He let Greensleeves take the lead.

10

AS ANOTHER big bear dropped, the golden aura of leveling enveloped Horc and the bold, gold text saying **Level 7** scrolled past.

Before he could comment on it, a quest popped up.

Quest: Speak to Caleb Sureshot
Go speak with Caleb Sureshot in Stone Helm City.
Rewards
XP: 100
Accept—Decline

Horc accepted. "Okay, just got a new quest to go speak with Sureshot, the Ranger trainer back in the city."

"You just hit level seven. I bet it's to get your companion quest," Greensleeves said as they started attacking another bear.

Letting another arrow fly, Horc frowned. "Companion quest? What's that?"

Baladara gave a heavy sigh as she hit the bear with enough magic to finish it off. "Have you noticed that all the Rangers who are standing around in the cities have animal companions with them?"

Horc thought about it as he checked the bear for loot. A few coppers and a pelt, something he needed for a quest he'd gotten from Brightbow at the camp when he turned in the wolf quest. "Okay, yeah. Sureshot has a big wolf, and I think Brightbow always has a bear next to him." He pulled out his knife and skinned the bear, getting his new skinning ability to rise another point. For the first time he got more than just useless scraps.

"Exactly. Their animal companions." Baladara bent over the carcass and pulled out something with a grin. "You know, I think running with you and your skinning profession makes my alchemical gathering easier. We can get twice the loot from the same corpse."

"Which is why it's good for people who frequently run together to have complementary professions," Greensleeves said. "Now roll this thing off the herb I need to get. I don't want to wait for the body to fade in a few minutes."

Horc heaved against the bloody bear and moved it enough so Greensleeves could get to the small flower that was covered in blood under it. He was still amazed by the lifelike realism the game incorporated. There was even a stench coming up from the bear that grew stronger when it was skinned, or when Baladara pulled parts off it.

Greensleeves offered the flower to Baladara. "I think you can probably use this." Since they'd gotten their professions on the last trip to town, Greensleeves had given all the herbs he collected to Baladara since she'd gotten a potions profession that allowed for both gathering of potion ingredients and crafting them into magical concoctions.

"Okay, so how soon do I have to head back to town for this quest?" Horc said as he pulled out another arrow and nocked it.

"We've got a few more bears on the leg of the chain." Baladara closed up her pack. "I say we finish this one and head back to town. Maybe you'll have enough cash to get another bag, or at least an expansion for one of the ones you've got."

"Yeah, I'm betting by the time we finish this quest, hand it and the other two in, we'll all be at level seven and ready for some training." Greensleeves headed deeper into the woods.

Horc sighed. "All this back and forth for training is a pain in the butt. Will we always have to go back to Stone Helm City for training? Sounds very inconvenient."

"As we go, we'll find new cities and they'll have other trainers and we won't have to go back to the same ones forever, just until we find some of the others." Baladara motioned for a stop and pointed up by a boulder at the base of a hill. Seconds later a big black bear lumbered into the open. **Black Bear, Level 7**

Having his bow ready, Horc managed to get the first shot off, before the two spell slingers got their attacks flying. The arrow buried itself in the bear's eye. The beast roared and stood up on two legs. Baladara and Greensleeves' attacks hit at the same time. They knocked the bear over onto its side. Horc's second arrow caught the bear in the heart. It shuddered and died. The three of them had worked out a good pattern of looting their kills. In less than a minute, they had it stripped bare and were off looking for their next target.

EVERY TIME Horc entered Stone Helm City, he was sure the place was getting more and more crowded. There seemed to be a ton of new Human players running around the cobblestone streets, almost all of them were level five or lower. They were increasing the background noise and he was amazed that most of them were running or jumping around the area, some with no apparent care for the other people around them.

"Hey," Baladara said as they reached the central square. "Do you two mind if I log out for a little while? Lisa's bugging me to get some rest and I think Horc's going to be okay for a little while. But, don't you guys go off and do the Gnoll dungeon without me. I want in on that."

"I can watch out for him," Greensleeves said. "Rick's going to let me know if I need to log out, but my pod should keep me going for a while."

"I think I can probably take care of myself," Horc objected.

Baladara shook her head. "You're still too much of a newb for us to leave you on your own and expect you to survive. I'll be back in a few hours. I know we're both off for the next two days, but I'm going to call the office and prepare them for the fact that if you're not out of your pod by then, I'm not going to be showing up."

Horc shook his head. "Don't do that. I really suspect I'll be out by Monday. But we also don't know what that kind of in-world time will do to me."

"We'll figure it out as it happens," Greensleeves said. "But there are people trying to get to you and save you IRL."

"I know, and you guys keep telling me that." Horc was a little agitated. "Not sure if it's all that helpful. Things are going to pan out the way they do. I'm trying to keep my mind off the real world right now by focusing on the game. Right now, unless they find my pod, or I really start to die, let's keep it on game stuff, okay?"

Both Baladara and Greensleeves nodded.

"Got it." Baladara grinned. "Okay. You two stay safe, I'll party chat you when I get back." Then Baladara faded from view.

"So, let's go see what this companion quest looks like," Horc said, heading toward Druid Park.

Greensleeves walked along beside him. "Sounds good. I figure I can use some training too. It's been a couple of levels since we've been here."

As they moved away from the central square and the vendors there, the number of players and their background chatter died down. There were still a few here and there, but most of the people around were NPCs.

The quiet lanes and cobblestone quaintness were beginning to grow on Horc. Sure, they were a lot different from the steel fabricated world of sci-fi games he was used to, but it had a certain charm he found himself enjoying. Depending on how things turned out, he might even play the game from time to time after the beta testing was done.

The scene in Druid Park was exactly as he remembered, only this time Caleb Sureshot was in one of the tents, sitting on a stool, fletching arrows. His large wolf lay curled up at his side.

When Horc walked in, Sureshot stood. "Ah, Horc, you got my message. I'm most impressed with the speed at which you are achieving your goals. It's time you learned more about being a Ranger." He gestured at a second stool across from the one he'd been sitting on. "Please, have a seat and we'll talk."

Not sure what would happen if he refused, Horc settled himself on the stool. It was the first time he'd been off his feet, other than being knocked down by attacking creatures, since he had entered the game. His feet throbbed and his back ached slightly. It still felt all too real.

Sureshot went back to fletching. "As a Ranger, you have a certain attachment to the world around us. Although we all work toward balance, we work differently than the Druids. Their way is more the way of the plants and growing things, while our way is the way of the animals we share the world with. They are more gentle and loving, while we understand the need for force." He picked up one of the arrows and jabbed it like he was trying to thrust it into some invisible prey. "We are their deadly hand when the need arises."

Having seen the devastating effects some of Greensleeves' spells could have, Horc wasn't exactly sure that was the case. But, he kept his mouth shut and listened to what Sureshot had to say.

"As each Ranger grows into their own power, they have to make choices, and find guidance. One of the ways we do that, is by taking animal companions. In the end, you'll have your choice of companions, and you may find that as you journey across Halfworld, you'll have need of different companions. But to begin this journey, I'll instruct you on how to gentle your first animals. Some Rangers do not complete the quests required to gain this skill. None will think any less of you should you fail, but you will find that your power will be enhanced by your companions."

It was sounding a bit convoluted, but Horc nodded. "I understand."

Sureshot smiled. "Good." He pulled out a blue charm. "I need you to take this charm and go find a black bear. Hold the charm out and don't feel fear as the beast attacks you. During his attack, you must not strike back against the bear. He's only doing what his instincts tell him to do. The magic of the charm takes a few seconds to work, but then the bear's attacks should lessen and stop all together. At that point the bear will be your companion."

Quest: Ranger Companion I
Requirements: Find one black bear and charm it into being your companion.
Rewards: 200 XP
Accept—Decline

Accepting, Horc took the charm. "And is that all for this quest?"

"When you complete the quest, return to me with your bear, and I'll give you the next step." Sureshot seemed to pause with an odd look on his face. He appeared to be waiting for Horc to say something.

"Thank you," Horc said and stood, tucking the charm in the front bag on his belt.

Sureshot nodded, then turned his attention back to the arrows.

Without another word, Horc walked out of the tent.

Greensleeves was standing there with his hands clasped in front of him. "That took a little while."

"That's the most he's talked on any of my quests so far," Horc said. "I've got to go charm a bear."

"Did he say where?" Greensleeves asked. "There's a fair number of bears in the woods near the city."

"I guess we can check the map once we clear the city walls." Horc started for the main gates.

"Good idea," Greensleeves said.

Not sure what it was going to feel like as a bear attacked him while he tried to charm it. Horc hoped Greensleeves would keep a healer's lock on him so if he dropped too low, he could be healed before he died.

11

"WHY DO quests care about where we go to do them, exactly?" Horc mumbled as they continued hiking south from Stone Helm City.

"Some games are more restrictive than others," Greensleeves said. "I think here in Halfworld, the game designers are trying to have us explore more. Who knows, this might all change after the beta. If people complain about quests being too hard, they'll go in and make them easier."

Horc shrugged. He wasn't exactly sure if his crankiness with the quest came from being trapped in the game, or something else. He'd been doing his best to not dwell on being trapped, maybe that was turning against him. "Let's see how this goes before I start filing complaints with the developers."

"Rick will appreciate that." Greensleeves paused and knelt down to pick an herb.

"Looks like we're finally in the right area," Horc said as he glanced at his map, they had just entered the red shaded zone that indicated they could find the bears in the area. He pulled out his bow and strung an arrow; even though he had the charm in his bag, he wanted to be ready in case the first bear they encountered was too strong for him.

"Okay. I'll make sure nothing takes you too far down." Greensleeves put the herb in his pack.

"Thanks." Horc stalked through the forest, scanning around for a black bear. From the way the other quests had gone, he knew the bears could be anywhere. He just hoped that since all he needed was one bear, there would be more than one in the area. The area the map indicated the bear might be in was fairly large, so there were lots of possibilities.

"You know, it would be nice if one of us had some kind of spell or ability to track animals. That'd be very useful." Horc swept the forest with his gaze.

"I can ask Rick to put that on the developers' table. That's one of the things this beta is for, to help make sure the game is the best it can be, and if that means new abilities and spells, then they'll see what they can do to improve things." Greensleeves flexed his hands, something Horc recognized as a tell that he was ready to cast a spell at a moment's notice.

"Anything I can do to help."

A limb cracked in the forest. Horc stopped and stared in the direction of the sound. Seconds later a large black bear lumbered into his view. **Black Bear, Level 9**

"I'll try this one." As it turned toward him, Horc dropped his bow and arrow to open his pack and pulled out the charm.

"I got your back," Greensleeves said.

The bear roared and charged. Horc held the charm out and did his best to not be afraid.

When the bear hit him, Horc flew through the air and hit a tree. Pain radiated across his back. Part of Horc wanted to pull his axe and attack the bear, but he resisted. He held the charm out and the bear hit him hard. His chest ached and his health bar dropped.

"Don't worry," Greensleeves said. "I've got you."

A healing glow enveloped Horc and his health bar returned to full as the bear hit him again. The healing didn't help the pain that went through him as the bear's claws raked the spot they had hit before. Horc screamed. He knew he couldn't attack the bear. He kept the charm out and continued to do his best to think positive thoughts.

The bear roared again and knocked him to the ground. It straddled him and sank its teeth deep into his shoulder. Horc screamed again.

Greensleeves healed him again. It seemed to do little to help Horc remain calm.

Seconds after his health maxed out, the bear tore a chunk out of Horc's shoulder. His health dropped by a half. Horc couldn't stay passive anymore. He hit the bear with the charm.

"I think this one is too strong." Horc tried to roll away as Greensleeves healed him again. The bear held him down.

A blast of green light struck the bear. It roared a third time and turned from savaging Horc. With the bear distracted, Horc hit it again. The bear's health bar started to drop.

"We've got to finish this thing quickly," Greensleeves said as another ball of green energy struck the bear. "My mana's almost drained."

Horc kicked up, trying to move the bear off him so he could stand and draw his axe.

The bear swiped at him. The pain in his shoulder was nearly unbearable. He scrambled away from the bear as it turned toward Greensleeves.

Struggling to his feet, Horc yanked his axe off his belt. He launched himself at the bear. With his axe he was able do more damage than he could with his hands. The bear glowed green as another bolt of Druid energy hit it. The beast's health bar was nearly half. It hit Horc again, forcing him back.

Swinging the axe as hard as he could, Horc managed to do a critical hit on the bear. Its health bar flashed red and it staggered as Greensleeves next bolt of magic struck. Its health bar gave a final slash and it dropped to the ground.

Horc got 150 experience, and his own health started flashing orange.

"Hey, how come I got 150 points for this bear? We've been averaging 50 points or so for our kills." Horc looted the bear. There were some coppers, a piece of bear meat, and a torn hide.

"Two things, we're not sharing the points with Baladara, and it was two levels above us." Greensleeves pulled out a flask and an apple.

"Really. So, there's a drawback to being in a party?" Horc asked as he set to skinning the bear.

"In addition to sharing loot, we share the XP," Greensleeves said. "But the safety of the party outweighs that. In some ways it slows down the leveling. I bet those moronic paladins were running together without being in a party so they could level faster."

Horc finished skinning and rolled up the leather he got so he could put it in his bag. "Since I didn't know any better, I figure things are going okay for me."

"I can't complain either." Greensleeves stood and dusted his leathers off. "We're accomplishing more together than we would separately."

"Okay then, let's see about finding a lower level bear," Horc said. "I'm guessing a lower level will be easier to charm."

"That's how it's supposed to work," Greensleeves said. "But you never know, sometimes the beasts get lucky."

"Then I won't try anything more than a level seven." Horc wanted to complete the quest, but didn't want to put himself at too much of a risk to do it.

"Sounds like a plan." Greensleeves put his flask away. "Let's take out anything above a seven, just to be safe."

"And avoid anything above a ten." Horc picked up his bow and arrow.

"Yeah, that's probably a good idea," Greensleeves said.

They set out and continued to go through the forest with the hopes of finding a low enough bear for Horc to take on. The next bear they encountered was a level eight. It took them several attacks to bring it down. By the time they killed it, Horc's health was half way down. He felt shaky. He wished Baladara was there, he didn't want to do something stupid and die, but then he stopped and thought about how many people died from doing stupid things, most of them just didn't die in video games.

After another three bears, they finally found a level seven. Horc made sure that his health was maxed out, and Greensleeves' mana was topped off. Then he slung his bow over his shoulder and pulled out the charm.

"Let's do this." Horc held the charm out and advanced on the bear. It felt different taking the fight to the bear as opposed to letting the bear come to him. He did his best to project positive feelings out through the charm. The bear reached him and Horc dodged. He was trying hard not to do anything aggressive. On the second swing, the bear caught him and knocked him backwards.

Horc's health bar dropped, but not as fast as it had with the more powerful bear. He held his ground and let the bear beat on him. His health kept dropping. Greensleeves healed him when he hit half. Horc braced himself for more pain. He really wanted to complete the quest and get his bear. As he lost another quarter of his health, the bear stopped attacking him. It backed up and stared at him, shaking its big shaggy head.

Horc kept the charm held out and kept thinking positive thoughts. The bear walked toward him. Horc tensed. Then the bear rubbed up against him like a huge cat.

Greensleeves laughed. "I guess it worked that time."

"I guess it did."

A new window popped up. It read **Companion Controls**. The only option in it was **Dismiss Companion**.

Horc looked at the bear who'd taken a seat next to him. He didn't want to dismiss the bear, he wanted to keep him. Plus, he was pretty sure Sureshot's quest had been to return with the bear. So far, he hadn't had any text roll past to indicate he'd completed the quest. He shook his head. "Okay, let's go back to town and see what Sureshot has to say. You guys said the companion can fight with us?"

Greensleeves nodded as they headed back toward the city. "That's right. It helps a Ranger do more damage. Just like some Druids can learn to shape change into animals if they want."

"Are you going to do that?" Horc rubbed the bear's head as they walked.

"I don't think so. I'm thinking about taking a Healer's talent tree, so that's different healer spells, and less combat stuff, but you never know; after the beta is over, I might want to try something a little different and do an Animage Druid just to see what it's like."

Horc continued rubbing the bear's head. "That sounds cool too. I guess there's still more to this fantasy gaming I've got to learn."

"It is a lot different from sci-fi gaming," Greensleeves said.

There wasn't any way Horc was even going to try to argue that. He just quietly hiked alongside his bear, heading back to town feeling a strange sense of accomplishment, even if he had come close to dying when he tried to charm the first bear that was way over his level.

12

TEXT INDICATING **Level 8** rolled down Horc's screen seconds after he turned in the quest to Sureshot. On the way back to town, he and Greensleeves had taken on a few monsters and having the bear along was almost as good as having Baladara with them casting spells. Seeing the companion in action made Horc think his chances of surviving until the rescuers got his pod out were improving.

As the leveling text vanished and Sureshot started talking again, the bear disappeared.

"Hey, wait a minute." Horc jumped to his feet, upsetting the stool he'd been sitting on. "Where did he go?"

Sureshot looked at him puzzled. "You have completed your quest for the bear. The bear you befriended has been returned to the forest where it belongs."

"I wanted to keep him." Horc righted the stool and plopped down on it. The bear had been the coolest thing in the game up to that point.

"When you complete the quests I have for you, you'll be able to charm all manner of beasts and can choose among them for your companion. Let us begin on the next quest quickly."

Horc barely heard the rest of the trainer's spiel as he laid out the next quest in the chain. He was numb when he accepted it. Even as he told himself he was stupid for getting upset over the loss of an animal that was just a bunch of pixels anyway, Horc knew, in his gut that when the quests were over, he'd go find himself another bear. Nothing would be as cool as a bear.

"OKAY, SO what is a Fire Roc anyway?" Horc asked as they reached the barren landscape signaling the desert where they were supposed to find the second animal he was supposed to charm. The map had the shaded area indicative of a quest zone.

"I checked while we've been walking and according to the wiki, it's a large vulture-like bird, but it can burst into fire." Greensleeves raised his hand and shaded his eyes. "They aren't supposed to be very common, though, so we might be searching for a while."

"Great." Horc mumbled. He was still feeling bad about losing the bear. He hadn't had it that long, and it didn't make any sense. He'd never really been a pet person. His life was full of work and trying to get financially stable. When he'd been a kid, his folks hadn't believed in pets, for similar reasons. It just felt odd to have an animal, even a digital one, walking calmly next to him and then helping him in a fight. He'd felt an almost instant connection with the bear and that didn't make any sense whatsoever.

They walked out across the desert. The heat coming off the brown sand made Horc think of summer in Dallas, but it was a much drier heat. The fact that game designers thought of that too impressed him even more with the game. He didn't get that level of realism in the games he was used to playing. After they left the forest, they'd spent all their time up to that point in, there had even been a warm breeze blowing in his face.

For several minutes they walked in a straight line from the point they'd entered the desert, heading south toward the heart of the shaded area after a few spots appeared in the cloudless blue sky.

"Hey, could those be what we're looking for?" Horc pointed toward the dots that were moving in lazy circles.

Greensleeves frowned. "Maybe. They're too far away to get a target lock on. Let's go over and find out. If they are, I wonder how hard it's going to be to pull just one, or if I'm going to have to deal with the flock while you try to charm one."

"No clue," Horc said, picking up his pace a little. He wanted to go find out if these were the Fire Rocs and see what level they were. The idea of taking on several creatures that were higher level didn't sound like a good one.

As they got closer, the dots became birds and Horc's hope that they were on the right track grew. Then the birds started dropping out of the sky and flying back up, like they were attacking something, or someone.

"They are Fire Rocs," Greensleeves said. "They look to be level seven to ten."

Horc shook his head. "Don't want to deal with a level ten."

"Right." Greensleeves started running. "They're after someone. We'd better get over there and see about getting yours before they're all gone."

"Sounds good." Horc ran after the Druid. Sand kicked up in their wake, leaving a cloud of dust in their passing. Horc had to move to the side slightly to avoid Greensleeves' dust.

When they topped a sand dune, the battle scene was obvious. A Fighter stood in the middle of the flock of Rocs. They were swinging a sword that looked too big to be functional in the real world. The birds kept hitting the Fighter.

Horc targeted the fighter to check them out. **Steelmaiden, Human, Barbarian, level 9**. Her health bar was dropping quickly with each hit from the birds.

"Greensleeves, see if you can heal her." Horc pulled out his bow and arrow and targeted one of the higher-level birds. "She's not in our party, so I don't know."

"Not a problem." Greensleeves cast a healing spell on the fighter as Horc fired his first arrow at a level ten roc.

Horc braced himself for an attack as he pulled out another arrow. The bird had already sustained damage and it didn't turn toward him but continued fighting Steelmaiden. His next arrow brought the bird out of the sky and it hit the ground so hard that dust billowed up where it landed.

He targeted two higher level birds and brought them down quickly.

"Go after that level seven over there." Greensleeves shouted. "I think I can cover both of you."

Steelmaiden hadn't acknowledged their presence, she seemed lost in her battle with the birds. She was a whirling blur of steel and flying red hair. Every time she brought down another bird, she screamed at the top of her lungs before swinging again.

Horc targeted the level seven bird. When he held up the charm toward it and started thinking calming thoughts like he'd done with the bear, the bird seemed to hover for a moment and then flew toward him. Its health bar was still full, and Horc wondered if it had attacked Steelmaiden yet. The ones who'd attacked her all seemed to have taken damage.

He didn't have long to ponder as the bird hit him hard in the head. He jerked back and had to focus to keep the charm going. The bird struck his upstretched arm. Horc nearly dropped the charm and reached up with his other hand to keep it from falling to the sand. His health had dropped to three quarters.

The blue glow of Greensleeves' healing spell engulfed him as the Fire Roc hit him again. Horc continued to hold up the charm, and really hoped it would work soon. His arm was getting tired.

Two more strikes, which were hard enough to make him stagger, but not hard enough to knock him into the sand, left him panting as Greensleeves healed him again. Then the roc hovered before him. It tilted its head and stared at him, then landed on his shoulder.

Grinning, Horc reached up and scratched its head. "Got him."

"Good, now let's finish the rest of these guys off before they finish off the Barbarian." Greensleeves cast another healing on the other player as Horc pulled his bow back out and took aim.

When the first arrow of his renewed attack struck a bird, the roc on his shoulder took off and joined the fight against that bird. With his companion helping, it only took Horc one more shot to finish off the attacking bird.

The last bird fell to the Barbarian and she roared before spinning around, obviously looking for the next bird. As her gaze passed over Horc, her eyes grew wide. She screamed something he couldn't understand and charged up the hill toward him.

Greensleeves cast some kind of spell and vines erupted out of the ground and caught her legs, jerking her to a stop. "Hold on there, lady. That bird's with us. We're the good guys."

She slashed at the vines, then paused and took a deep breath. "Oh. Sorry." Her voice had a thick Irish lilt to it. "When I aggroed too many of those things I activated my Battle Fury and got lost in the haze. Thanks for the healing."

Horc frowned. "Aggroed? Battle Fury?"

Steelmaiden chuckled. "Are you a newb? Aggro is when you pull a mob of some sort. Battle Fury is what this game calls berserker rage. It's one of the special attacks for a Barbarian."

"Ah." It made sense now that Horc heard it. "So the whole flock attacked at once?"

Steelmaiden slid her humungous sword into its scabbard on her back. "Right. Nasty things. Not sure why you'd want one for a pet."

Horc shrugged. "Quest. I haven't exactly figured out what I want for a companion yet, but I did like the bear I got in the first quest." He scratched the Fire Roc again and just didn't get the same feeling of contentment he had from petting the bear.

"Ah, that makes sense then." She brushed dust off her leather armor. "Have you got other quests in this area?"

Greensleeves shook his head. "Not yet. We're going to do the Gnoll dungeon after we finish the companion quests, and a friend of ours rejoins us."

"I've heard from a couple of players who've tried it, that it's impossible at suggested level. They said they were going to level a bit more before trying it again. Maybe three or four levels above might make it doable."

"Is that what you're trying to do?" Horc asked. "Get up higher before trying it again?"

Steelmaiden nodded. "Yeah. Most of the people I've run into so far have been complete sods so I had to tell them to bugger off. I figure if I'm high enough, I can do it on my own." She sighed and started looting the rocs. "Also trying to get some extra cash for better gear."

"Sounds like a good plan," Greensleeves said. "Hey, we're down a party member right now, would you care to join us? Once we finish Horc's companion quests, we're just going to do a bit of farming to XP, and loot while we wait for Baladara to log back in. Maybe by then we'll be ready for the dungeon."

"We promise we're not complete pricks," Horc said. "That is if you don't mind running with a Half-Orc."

Steelmaiden laughed. "I honestly thought about doing either a Half-Elf or a Half-Orc myself. The extra bits about trying to balance your character sounded interesting, plus the bonuses a Half-Orc Barbarian gets are incredible. Half Orcs are the best race for Barbarians, but I opted for Human since I figured most of the folks from the office were going to run Humans and we might be able to get together in-game. So far, all I've run into are some prats from marketing."

"I think I ran into those fools," Greensleeves said. "Complete bullies."

"Sounds like them," Steelmaiden said. "Sure. Send me a Party Invite and let's get this going. We can take out monsters as we go back to town, I guess if you're going to turn in a Ranger quest it'll be in town."

Horc nodded and turned back toward town. "That's right." Having another member in their party made sense as it would improve his chances of living until his pod could be retrieved. "Ah, how do we add her to the party? Mike…ah…Baladara set up the group originally."

Greensleeves got a faraway look. "Ah, according to the interface, Horc, you're now group leader, at least until Baladara comes back. Target Steelmaiden then right click on her avatar. You should get a dropdown window."

Horc did as he suggested. He had several options in the small, new window. "Okay, now what."

"Select *Invite*," Greensleeves instructed.

As soon as Horc did it, Steelmaiden's info showed up under Greensleeves's.

"There we go," Steelmaiden said. "Now let's see what we can get done. It'd be nice to put on a few more levels today."

"Totally with you there," Greensleeves said.

They turned and started back the way they'd come, keeping their eyes open for any creatures they might be able to take out on the way. With the companion, they had a four member party, and were able to make quick work of any solo monsters they came across. Several times they'd headed a short distance off the main road to take on flocks of rocs. Combined with a scattering of scorpions and a couple of large rattlesnakes, they kept racking up XP. By the time they returned to Stone Helm City, they'd each put on another level, and had a fair amount of loot.

13

HORC LET out a long breath as he finished charming the wolf he'd been sent after. They were in the area near the Gnoll dungeon but unlike the previous wolves they'd killed in the zone earlier, the Massive Wolves had been level ten and attacked with a pack of five. If he hadn't had Greensleeves and Steelmaiden with him, he never would've completed the quest. Having had the rocs and wolves both attack as a mob, and not being able to pull just one without aggroing the whole pack or flock, made it hard.

The wolf came over to him the way the bear had. It sniffed him, then licked his hand that was still holding the charm out. The beast huffed, then sat down at his feet.

"A little help here would be appreciated," Greensleeves said from a short distance away where he and Steelmaiden were still fighting the last two pack members.

"Oh, sorry." Horc targeted the biggest of the two wolves and fired two arrows in quick succession. The wolf at his side jumped up and launched itself at the wolf and in seconds it went down.

Horc turned his attention to the final wolf as Steelmaiden brought her gigantic sword down hard on the beast, crushing its skull and leaving it lying on the ground.

Steelmaiden wiped her brow with the back of her hand. "Wow, that would've been impossible for one player all by their lonesome. I totally don't get this. Why make the quests so hard?"

"We'll need to fill out reports and get them to the designers so they can tweak things," Greensleeves said as he stooped to loot the wolf closest to him.

"I guess that is the point of a beta run, isn't it?" Steelmaiden looted the wolf she'd just brought down. "Okay, so since we've got this one done, can we venture a little farther into the zone and get the wolf I need for my level ten quest? It's supposed to have extra loot."

"Sure, we're in the area," Horc said. "Let's get it down and done with. So, if it's a level ten quest for you, what extra do you get? I think I understand my companion quest and me getting a companion."

She got a faraway look for a moment, then turned and pointed to the south east. "It's that way. What I get out of this quest is the ability to call a wolf to help me fight for one minute. That's one of the perks to the Barbarian, as we go up in level we can call animals to help us in our fights. They don't stick around like your companions do, but they help out for a minute. In the middle of a big battle the right animal coming to help can really turn the tide. It's something Halfworld is pulling from other games, but then a lot of the genre games have the same things from one game to another, they just change the names or levels, or something to make it a little bit different."

"Okay. Sounds cool." Horc followed her and Greensleeves as they hiked through the forest heading toward the next quest. The more he learned about the game, the more he liked it. He tried to remember what it was about fantasy games in the past that he hadn't liked but couldn't really recall exactly. He'd tried several, they all seemed similar in his mind. Maybe that was it, there was too much in each game that was close to other games in the genre. Everything was Humans, Elf, Dwarf, or some variation on that with Fighters, Mages, Priest and the like. Halfworld had a wide variety of things with various possibilities even after a player chose his or her race and class. He wanted to spend some time researching the Ranger on the wiki, and thought that maybe after they reached town for some down time, he'd get Greensleeves to show him how to get into it so he could research. Since they were still in beta, he figured the wiki was still fairly basic and waiting for characters to help fill in the gaps, but it would give him a way to make semi-informed decisions on the direction he wanted to take his toon.

Steelmaiden held up her hand, signaling a stop. "Map shows a cave just over the next ridge. He should either be in there or somewhere nearby."

"Lead the way." Greensleeves shook out his hands.

Horc nocked an arrow as they all crept forward toward the cave. Doing their best to not warn the wolf of their presence they worked around the mouth of the cave. There were footprints in the dirt outside of the cave. Here and there bones were scattered around, a sure sign a large predator was nearby.

"I can't get a target on anything." Steelmaiden edged closer to the cave. "Let's slip in and see if it's in there."

The cave was tight, so Horc shouldered his bow and pulled his axe. He didn't think he had room to shoot arrows and hoped the wolf companion he had would be enough to counter not having his bow.

They took each step carefully as they went deeper into the cave. The number of bones on the ground increased. Horc gripped his axe and kept it at the ready.

A deep growl was all the warning they had, then the wolf was on Steelmaiden. She swung her sword and the wolf slid under the attack.

Greensleeves hit it with a bolt of druid energy.

Above the wolf the text read **Cave Wolf level 12** there was a star next to the text.

Horc swung his axe hard. "What does the star mean?"

"It's a special creature." Greensleeves got another bolt of energy off. "More dangerous."

With a howl of anger, Horc's companion wolf joined the fight. It launched itself at the Cave Wolf. The two canines clashed in the middle of the cave in a mass of snarling fur and fangs.

Steelmaiden swung her sword and hit the cave wolf. Its health bar flashed and the combined damage dropped it a third of its health.

Greensleeves hit it again with another blast of druid magic.

The wolf yelped and backed up.

Horc's wolf pressed his attack as Horc and the others pressed theirs. They dropped the wolf down to half. It stopped backing up and rushed them. It caught Horc and knocked him to the ground. The blow knocked a quarter out of Horc's health. Gasping for breath, he swung his axe as hard as he could. It took a good chunk out of the wolf's life as Steelmaiden next blow connected.

Greensleeves's magic attack hit again. "Guys, I'm not doing much against this thing."

"I think it might have some kind of anti-magic buff," Steelmaiden suggested. "Your attacks have always been a lot more effective than this."

She jumped onto the wolf's back as it chomped down on Horc's leg.

"Then heal us!" Horc shouted as his health dropped to almost half. He wondered how the wolf was managing to do so much damage so quickly, but it was three levels higher than he was and had the special star. He wondered if it was attacking him because he was the lowest level of the three of them.

Aiming for the beast's head, he hit it as hard as he could. The axe sank into the wolf's head. Its health sank and Greensleeves's spell encompassed Horc in its blue light, returning his health to almost normal. Steelmaiden's next attack drove its health even lower.

Pain tore through Horc as the wolf twisted his leg. There was a loud snap and a wave of agony shot through Horc's leg and into his hip. He screamed and his health bar dropped to just below half.

Horc's companion wolf tore at the bigger wolf. The monster's health continued to fall. The blue glow of Greensleeves's spell engulfed Horc before his scream died down. The healing did nothing for the pain he felt even as he knew the leg was completely healed. He hit the wolf again at the same time as Steelmaiden.

The wolf's health flashed red and it scrambled to get away. Steelmaiden's next blow was the final. The Cave Wolf collapsed and she gave a triumphant shout. "Yes!"

Greensleeves sighed as he walked over to gather some mushrooms from the cave wall. "That's not something I would've wanted to try to handle on my own. Together we managed to get it down."

"Which is why it's a good idea to have a party." Steelmaiden wiped down her sword. "We can tackle higher level mobs. And this would've been way too strong for me to take on by myself. I managed to get my quest objective and another level. Thanks guys. It's nice to find guys who aren't complete sods."

"So where do you turn it in at?" Horc asked.

"To the north of the Stone Helm City gate, there's a small camp of Barbarians. I turn the quests in there, and the trainer is there." Steelmaiden slipped some meat into her bag as coins clinked in all their bags.

Horc bent to skin it. At the point he normally would've had the leather, a message popped up.

Skinning attempt failed.

Try again.

"What?" Horc tried again. Again, the message popped up. "Okay, why can't I skin this thing?"

"Your skinning skill must not be high enough for it." Greensleeves put the mushrooms into his pack.

"Okay, so I guess that's more like the higher-level creatures kicking my butt?" Being stubborn, Horc tried again and got the message as the wolf carcass faded away into digital bits.

"Yeah, exactly like that," Steelmaiden said. "But don't worry, the way we're slaughtering mobs right now, you'll get your skinning up to a higher level anytime now."

"Leveling, this game is all about being a higher level, isn't it?" Horc wiped his axe off with a scrap of leather he pulled from his pack.

"That's a big part of it," Greensleeves said. "You're supposed to have a grand adventure, but overall, you get more done by leveling."

Horc noticed that his wolf companion was limping and its health bar only had a quarter left. "Is there any way to heal my wolf?"

"Try feeding it," Steelmaiden suggested. "That works in some other games, or when you get to a certain level, you can heal it yourself. It's a benefit for the pet."

After digging a piece of meat out of his bag, Horc tossed it to the wolf. The wolf caught it before it hit the ground. He chewed it up, but its health didn't go up.

Horc frowned. "What now?"

"Maybe it's because this isn't a permanent companion," Greensleeves suggested. "Something that would work for a permanent pet might not work on a quest pet."

His answer made Horc remember that this pet like the other two was going to fade away when he turned in the quest. Although the roc hadn't made a big impact on him, the bear and the wolf had. He'd felt a real connection with them. He didn't want the wolf to fade away into nothing. It had been hard enough when the bear did. The wolf had injured itself helping Horc and his party. It made a huge impact on him. If this was the final part of the quest chain, he wondered if he could ask Sureshot to let him keep the wolf. It had proven it would be a good companion.

"Let's head on back to town," Horc suggested. "Let's get the quests turned in and see what's next."

Greensleeves nodded. "Sounds good."

Horc hoped they didn't run into anything they might have to fight. He didn't want the wolf's health to drop too far. He wanted it to be okay.

CALEB SURESHOT was sitting outside his tent near the communal fire in Druid Park when Horc walked up with the wolf stalking next to him. Greensleeves strolled over to the Druid trainer without a word.

"Ah, young Ranger, you have completed your companion quests." Caleb Sureshot set aside the piece of leather armor he'd been mending.

"I have something to ask you." Horc knew Sureshot was just an NPC, so he wasn't sure how the trainer would react. Regardless if he had a proper answer or not, Horc had to find out. He had no idea what would happen if he tried to change the quest. "So, instead of this one just fading away like the other two did, is there any way I could keep him?"

For a moment, Sureshot stared at him, as if trying to find the right answer. It was like the AI in charge of the game hadn't expected the question and wasn't sure how to respond. Then he blinked and reached down to pet his own wolf curled at his feet. "The bond between a Ranger and his companion is a sacred thing. You are both willing to lay down your lives for each other. What you ask is unusual. Normally when a Ranger completes his companion quests, he goes out into the world and finds himself a new pet."

"But couldn't an exception be made? Is there a reason why I have to go out and find another companion when this one will do me just fine?" Horc told himself that it was stupid for him to plead with a bit of coding. Sureshot had a set number of responses. He couldn't go beyond them.

"It is a fine wolf." Sureshot nodded. "It is indeed." He made a mystical pass with his hand. "You will have to charm him again, but he will not fade away before you have a chance to do so."

Horc grinned. "Thank you."

"Do you wish to complete the quest?" Sureshot asked.

Horc nodded. "Yes."

The quest completed and text on his screen informed him that he had acquired a new skill, charming creatures. There were several other abilities related to it that scrolled past his screen.

Horc brought up the new ability and instantly used it on the wolf he'd come into town with. It wasn't like the last time he'd cast the charm on the wolf. It didn't attack him. It just stood there and stared at him then it walked over and sat at his feet.

Tears rolled down Horc's face as he stroked the wolf's head.

After a moment, Greensleeves rushed over. "Okay, now it's my turn for the major quest. Let's get Steelmaiden and head off into the woods."

Horc nodded. "Let's get it done. Thanks for helping me with the companion quests. I wouldn't have made it through without you and Steelmaiden."

"That's what parties of friends are for, right?"

"Right." Horc wondered if any of them would still be friends after he found a way out of the game. They lived away from each other, but he knew friendships were more than just being physically close to each other. He didn't have a lot of friends IRL but seeing how they were very helpful in the game world, he wondered if he should make more of an effort to know more people in the real world too.

14

"SO, WHAT'S the quest?" Horc asked as the three of them turned away from the city and headed into the forest.

"It actually ties into the Gnoll dungeon." Greensleeves led the way. "I'm supposed to find a group of adventurers and save them from some Ice Bears and Gnolls on the mountain above the dungeon. They are all badly wounded and in need of healing. Only a strong healer can do the quest."

Steelmaiden chuckled as they hiked along. "Isn't that always how it is with these quests?" She dropped the tone of her voice and sounded ominous. "Only the strong can complete the quest, only the brave of heart will be able to survive the horrible jungle." She returned her voice to normal. "Sometimes I think we need to get real writers to come in and help the game designers do their job. The game designers handle the techie end of things and the writers get the storylines and dialogue done right so it doesn't sound so cheesy."

"We can post that as a suggestion," Horc said. "Maybe that's been one of the things I prefer about the sci-fi games. They lack the cheesy quality."

"Ah, but come on, sometimes the cheese is the tastiest part of the game," Greensleeves said.

Horc groaned and resisted the urge to slug him.

Beside Horc, his wolf growled as if he understood every word and hadn't liked it either.

"What do you get out of this quest?" Steelmaiden asked.

"A new powerful healing spell, and a shape-changing spell that lets me become an Ent with even greater healing power." Greensleeves stared up the trail they were following. "But it's not supposed to be an easy quest, so this time you two get to lay down cover for me while I get the lost party healed and on their feet away from here."

"As long as the mobs aren't too high level, this shouldn't be too hard," Steelmaiden said.

"Exactly," Greensleeves added. "I think with the three of us…four if we count the wolf, should be able to do this without too much trouble.

Horc hoped he was right. Greensleeves's attention was going to be on his quest more than it was on the party. If things got too rough, they could all die.

They skirted the area where they'd been killing pigs earlier, then headed up into the mountains near where they'd gotten the quests for bear skins and such. Not being on the road, the terrain was steep and their going was slow. Several times they had to pause to battle a bear, or wolf that crossed their path, but none of it were things they couldn't handle.

Halfway up the mountain, they came across their first Gnoll. The red text above its head, that was more canine than anything else, read **Gnoll Scout, level 10**.

Steelmaiden charged in at it as if she didn't care about anything other than killing the thing that looked like an odd cross between a coyote and a human. She shouted and drew its attention.

Horc fired his first arrow and when it struck the monster, his wolf leapt into action. Between the four of them, they made short work of the beast, and when it was done, it rewarded them with 100 XP and a handful of copper.

"Don't really expect a whole lot out of these guys until we head into the dungeon," Steelmaiden said as she dusted off her hands and used the Gnoll's torn leather shirt to clean her blade.

"Why should that make much difference?" Horc asked as he nocked another arrow to be ready is something else snuck up on them.

"We don't know for sure about Halfworld, but in most other games, the drops are bigger in dungeons than they are just out wandering around." Steelmaiden dropped the Gnoll's shirt over its unmoving face. "There's going to be more high-level or powerful mobs and we'll have to be ready for a fight."

Horc frowned as he scanned the forest. "Then is it a good idea for me to do it? I mean, I might die."

Steelmaiden laughed. "Sweetie, everyone dies in games. It's just a matter of fact. Don't worry about it so much, or you won't be able to enjoy yourself."

Greensleeves shook his head. "Horc, we haven't told her about your situation yet. How you're a special case right now."

She stopped and looked at Horc as she combed her fingers through her long red hair.

"Yeah, we haven't." Horc said. He quickly took time to lay out the situation for her so she'd understand what was going on.

"Well, crap," Steelmaiden said after Horc finished explaining. "Knowing that, I'm not sure it's a good idea to take you into a dungeon, even a beginner level one like the Gnoll King's Lair."

"If we wait for Baladara, we should be fine," Greensleeves said. "Other than her, we'll all be over basic level for the incident, so there shouldn't be too much of a problem. With Steelmaiden and your wolf tanking, you and Baladara as DPS, and me handling healing, we should be fine. Who knows? We might even run into a solo or two on the way in who want a party to take the dungeon on with and that'll improve our chances even more."

Horc sighed and rubbed his wolf between its ears. "You make it sound easy." He hoped Greensleeves wasn't blowing too much smoke.

"Yeah, he does," Steelmaiden agreed. "But he could very well be right, particularly if we put on a few more levels before your friend gets back."

Another level ten Gnoll Scout appeared. They stopped talking for a moment while they dispatched it. It seemed to go down faster than the first one had. Horc checked his XP bar: after the last kill, he was about halfway to level ten. But if the dungeon was going to be filled with harder mobs, he wanted to be a lot higher than that before they went in.

"So where are these blokes who need healing supposed to be?" Steelmaiden asked as she stared around the forest.

"We've entered the area of my map shaded for them, but I'm not totally sure." Greensleeves leaned on his staff and scanned the woods too. "Since it's a fairly decent sized piece of the mountain side, I bet they're scattered. If it was just a small encampment, there'd probably be either a dot or much smaller shaded portion on the map."

Something moved near the base of a tree. Horc peered and was a little surprised when it looked like a human who'd tried to cover himself up with some leaves. The text above the man read **Wounded Adventurer, Human, Level 10**. His health bar was nearly empty.

"Is that one?" Horc pointed toward the man at the base of the tree.

Greensleeves grinned. "Yes, it is." He hurried over to the man with Horc and Steelmaiden following close behind him. He knelt next to the man. "I'm here to help you." The blue of his healing spell engulfed the man.

As the healing glow faded, the adventurer stood, then gave Greensleeves a short bow. "Thank you for healing me, brave Druid. I knew the Druids would send someone to help us. I knew they wouldn't leave us to rot. I must run warn the king. He has to know the evils that spawn in the borders of his kingdom."

"Please let the king know quickly," Greensleeves said. "Take care as you go through the forest—there are a lot of vicious creatures out there."

The man nodded and then hurried off.

"That's one." Greensleeves looked around. "Now, let's find the other nine."

Having realized what he was looking for, Horc had something to focus on as they went through the forest. There were more Gnolls and the occasional Ice Bear attacking them every few feet. It was like they had completely taken over the forest. Of all the monsters he'd encountered in the game, their population was the densest. It made him wonder what they would be like once they got into the dungeon.

"Look out!" Steelmaiden rushed toward the tree Horc stood near.

His wolf growled and charged the same direction.

Horc looked the way they ran. Sunlight glittered off steel. Gut instinct told him to drop. He hit the ground and rolled as a huge Gnoll swung its sword at him. When he stopped rolling, he got a look at the creature's text. **Gnoll Guard, level 15**. It included a star on the end.

Pulling his axe, Horc swung hard and sank the blade into the Gnoll's leg. His wolf caught the Gnoll in the back, it staggered and nearly fell over Horc. A green glow hit the Gnoll and forced it backwards.

Steelmaiden shouted her War Cry and cut the Gnoll deep. The damage had barely begun to register on its health bar.

Horc hit at the Gnoll again. He wished Baladara was there—they needed every member of their party. The wolf hit the Gnoll again. It grabbed the monster by the hand and yanked it hard.

With a roar of pain and anger, the Gnoll hurled the wolf against a tree. The wolf yelped from pain and its health bar dropped to half.

"No!" Horc shouted and cut the Gnoll again. He wasn't sure what to do. He hit the Gnoll again, then remembered something either Greensleeves or Steelmaiden had said. He pulled up his ability list and frantically looked for something that would help. He wanted—no, needed to help his wolf.

Another blast from Greensleeves hit the Gnoll. It slashed at the wolf with its claws. The wolf yelped again, and Horc hit the Gnoll hard, hoping his actions didn't close his character window so he could keep looking for a spell, or an ability that would help.

The wolf's health dropped again.

Horc spotted an ability for Companion Healing. He activated the ability. For several seconds, he couldn't do anything else as the energy welled up in him and went to the wolf. Then the wolf's health went up.

When the casting time of the ability was up, it went gray on his character sheet and began a countdown. Horc was slightly lightheaded. He wasn't sure if it was from healing the wolf, or from the damage he was taking as the Gnoll had turned on him.

"Why are you things always picking on the little guy?" Anger welled up in Horc. He swung his axe for all he was worth. The axe hit hard and cleaved the Gnoll's arm.

It howled in pain, sounding like the bipedal coyote it looked like. Its health bar dropped to just a quarter.

"Way to crit the thing!" Steelmaiden shouted and hit the monster hard.

Another hit by Greensleeves and it was down. **150 XP** flashed.

"Wow, that's some good XP," Greensleeves said.

Horc hugged his wolf. In that moment, it didn't matter that his companion didn't exist outside the game. The wolf was very much real, and Horc had come close to losing it. He opened his pack and pulled out a chunk of meat and handed it to the wolf. As the wolf ate it, the bit of health that hadn't gone up after Horc's healing came back.

"Okay. Let's try not to stumble on those things again," Horc said. "That was too close."

Steelmaiden stared at him from where she'd started looting the Gnoll. "What? You didn't drop below three quarters. If you're going to take the not dying thing so seriously you might want to just go back to the city and belly up to the bar until you've been rescued."

"It wasn't me." Horc glared at her as coins clinked into his purse. "My wolf nearly died."

"Okay. You know that's not really a big deal don't you?"

"Just because I can go out and get another one, it's not a big deal? Don't things matter in this game?" Horc tried to understand what he was hearing, but it hurt. He'd come too close to losing the wolf.

Greensleeves touched his arm. "No, I don't think that's what she's getting at here. Check your spells and abilities. It's probably under companion stuff."

"Like where I found the healing spell?" Horc brought his character sheet back up and started going through things again. It was easier without the Gnoll attacking them. There were a series of options there. The count down for the healing spell was nearly over. Below the healing spell was one for Revive Companion. There were also options for Charm Companion, Release Companion.

Horc sighed. "I'm sorry I got snappy, Steelmaiden. I don't know why I'm getting so attached, and when I thought I was about to lose the wolf, I stressed out. I see now I can revive it if it dies. I'm guessing it'd be the same wolf, and not just some random computer-generated wolf, right?"

Steelmaiden pursed her lips and for a moment looked at Horc like he was crazy. "You know, I don't think anyone has ever wondered that before."

"I'll have to ask Rick about that," Greensleeves said. "I bet it's something he's never heard of either, but maybe it's something they can incorporate into the game to make it more personal. Maybe if companions could get customized somehow, like with special armor or even collars—players would like that."

"That might be really cool." Horc scratched his wolf on the ear and it acted like there was nothing wrong, and never had been. In his mind, he knew it was just a string of code and pixels, but it felt and acted so real. There was no way he could treat it like it was just some random numbers the computer generated. "I wonder if I can give it a name."

"Maybe. Not sure they have that functionality yet." Greensleeves walked over to a tree and pulled some bark off of it and put the bark in his pack. "If they haven't, then we request it."

"How can I figure that out?" Horc asked.

In the distance, another Gnoll howled.

"Tell you what—let's figure that out back in town," Steelmaiden said as she turned toward the sound. "We don't need to get caught by surprise again."

"Definitely." Horc closed his character sheet. He pulled out his bow, nocked an arrow and was ready when another Gnoll appeared from behind a tree a short distance away. Determined to make sure it didn't hurt either his wolf, or other party members, he fired as fast as he could while the others also attacked the monster. It howled as it rushed them. It had no way to damage them without being in close range. By that time, they already had it down to half. Horc dropped his bow and yanked out his axe. He attacked the Gnoll as furiously as he could. He didn't even care that it came at him. He wanted to draw its attention so the others could do their work. It dropped quickly and they could loot it.

"You don't have to do that," Steelmaiden said as she cleaned her blade.

"Do what?" Horc asked, really starting to feel like she was just being overly critical of almost everything he did.

"Draw aggro on yourself like that." She took up a defensive stance as Greensleeves finished looting the corpse and copper clinked into Horc's bag. "I'm our tank. You and Greensleeves are DPS. If you really want to stay alive, let me draw the mobs' attention. I can take more damage than you can. Don't go off and get all macho man on me. Just because I'm a girl doesn't mean I can't fight."

Horc shook his head. "That wasn't it at all. I wanted to kill it before it had a chance to do much damage."

"Which is all well and good," Greensleeves said. "But she's right. That's what tanks are for in fantasy games…sort of like space marines in sci-fi games. Let them rush in while we stand back and shoot. I'll keep an eye on everyone's health while I'm blasting things. You can watch the wolf's health. When we get back to town, I'll show you how to set up quick cast options to make sure you don't have to go digging for the healing and anything else you think you might need."

"Still figuring this all out," Horc said. "I'm starting to think I'm going to be a newb at this game forever."

Greensleeves laughed and tossed a bow to Horc. "I doubt that. See if this is any better than the one you have."

Horc looked at the bow.

Bow of the Forest

Damage 12-15

Speed 6

His old bow read

Apprentice Ranger Bow

Damage 1-4

Speed 3

"Thanks, it's a definite improvement," Horc said as he put the old bow in his bag and equipped the new one.

"You're the only one of us who uses a bow. It makes sense," Greensleeves said. He tossed a handful of arrows to Horc. "You might need these too. Looks like you forgot to get more when we were in town again."

Horc closed his eyes and resisted the urge to sigh. There was just so much to remember and it got overwhelming after a little bit.

"We've got another one a few trees down," Steelmaiden said. "I'm going to charge it. You guys be ready to follow up right after I hit it."

Before they had a chance to reply, she charged toward the Gnoll. They were left with no option but to get ready to blast away. Horc was amazed at how light and comfortable the new bow felt in his hands. When he let loose his arrow, it moved faster than any arrow he'd shot before. When it struck the Gnoll, it knocked the monster back a couple of feet and its health dropped to three quarters.

"I like this bow!" He strung another arrow and fired again. His second shot hit at the same time as Greensleeves's Druid magic and his wolf. The Gnoll was at half health. It howled. Steelmaiden hit it hard again. Horc hit it twice for each blow Greensleeves got in. It felt great as the Gnoll's health bar flashed red and it fell to the ground.

"Wow. If I'd known a better bow was available, I would've tried to find one in town." He slung the bow over his shoulder and went to help with the looting.

Movement near the base of another tree caught his attention. It was just like the first Adventurer they'd found. "Greensleeves, over there." He pointed at the injured man.

"Thanks." Greensleeves hurried over to the man. "I wish these guys showed up on my map the way the herbs do."

"You're asking them to make things too easy, you know that." Steelmaiden laughed. "Horc, you might stop in at the flea market and see what they have in the way of better weapons and armor. It's a good idea to do that every few levels so you don't end up going on forever with apprentice gear."

"Sounds like a good idea." Horc did a quick heal on the wolf. It had sustained a little damage. Then for good measure, he pulled out a chunk of meat and gave it to him.

Greensleeves came back over as the healed Adventurer ran off through the woods. "That's two. Boy, this quest is taking forever."

Steelmaiden shrugged. "No worries. We need the XP and the loot's not bad either. At least, humanoids drop more cash and such than creatures."

"Okay then, let's continue on." Greensleeves gestured to the forest and Horc and Steelmaiden followed, on guard for the next Gnoll or fallen adventurer.

15

AS THEY walked into Stone Helm City, Horc realized that his feet hurt and he was more tired than he could ever remember being while in his pod, in a game. He'd made it to level ten, nearly to eleven. The others had made it to level twelve.

He yawned. "Hey, I'm whooped. Is this normal?"

Greensleeves paused. "Wow. We've been playing for nine hours. I think we're due for a rest."

"You guys must be in pods… well, I know Horc is." Steelmaiden said.

"We both are," Greensleeves said. "How about you?"

Steelmaiden nodded. "Me too, but honestly, I think I could use a little down time. Even in pods, too much game time can get to be a problem if we aren't careful."

"My husband's one of the game designers," Greensleeves said. "He's making sure to keep an eye on my pod and my vitals. He'll pull me out if it gets to be a problem. But I should probably get some in-game shut eye if nothing else."

"But none of us have houses," Horc said. "Are we supposed to go to an inn or something?"

"Exactly," Steelmaiden said. "Maybe if we take some down time, by the time your friend logs back in, we'll be ready to hit the forest again. Come on you guys, let's go find the inn and hope it isn't too expensive."

Horc had never heard of taking rest time in a game, but it made sense. He figured if he kept going as tired as he was he was going to start making mistakes and that would make it hard for everyone.

WHILE GREENSLEEVES started snoring from the other bed in the room, Horc sat on the side of his bed and stared at the text box he'd brought up. It was early morning in Dallas, and he was sure his mother had probably heard the news by then. He was a little surprised he hadn't received texts from her frantic, but there wasn't anything from anyone. He just hoped the connection to the cell network was still working, but figured if he was still in the game, something kind of communications network was still working.

With a shaking hand, he frowned and started a text to his mother. He kept is fairly simple and direct.

Mom, I'm okay. I was in my game pod when the storm hit. I'm buried in the pod, but still alive. The company knows where I am and is working to reach me.

As he waited for a response, he pulled off his boots.

A soft chime rang in his ears.

Alan, what do you mean you're buried after a storm hit?

Haven't you seen the news yet? A tornado went through my neighborhood last night. Took out my house. He couldn't believe she hadn't seen what happened.

OMG. Your father and I called it an early night last night and we haven't turned on the news yet. But you're okay?

Horc lay back on the bed. *I'm stuck in the game I was playing. At this point my game pod is keeping me alive. So it really depends on how you define okay.* He started to wish his pod could hook up with voice on his phone, but they didn't have that functionality. It might be something to request to be added in the future.

There it is. OMG. The news says thousands are dead.

That's what I heard. Horc's hands started to cramp slightly from the odd angle of the keyboard. He swiped the texting to speech.

At least you're not one of them. Should we head to Texas?

No. Stay in Arizona unless your ready to head to Maine for the summer. Horc figured the last thing the rescuers needed were his folks trying to help get to him.

Maybe next week. Your father has a gold prospecting class he wants to go to before we head home.

Then go enjoy that. I'll try to keep you posted about what's going on with me, and let my friends know to contact you if something bad happens. The only person he had to do that was Mike. Horc paused and stared out the dark window of the Inn room he'd rented. He never stopped to realize how few friends he really had. The only one he really trusted to let his family know if something happened to him was Mike, or one of the supervisors at work. That was really pathetic.

But nothing's going to happen, right?

Right, Mom. I need to go. I love you. Tell Dad to enjoy his class.

I will. You stay safe. We love you.

I'll do my best. Not wanting to drag the conversation out too long and get too mushy, Horc closed the window and put his arms behind his head. Before he fell asleep, he pulled up another text window and sent Mike a message with how to contact his folks if something should happen. He hated doing it, but he had to. He knew his life was hanging on by a string and all he could do was play a game and hope rescuers got to him in time.

"I CAN'T believe I disappear for a little while and you guys put on levels and then crash." Baladara's voice woke Horc from the comfortable bed he was asleep in. "I got your message by the way. I'll handle anything I have to."

"Thanks." Horc blinked at her. "How did you find us?"

"When I logged on, I looked at the map and it showed me where my party was." She crossed her arms and glared. "And you added to the party. Barbarians make pretty good tanks. Is he any good?"

"She's good." Horc sat up and rubbed his eyes. On the other bed in the small room, Greensleeves was doing the same.

"Looks like it's light outside," Greensleeves said. "So at least we got some rest."

Baladara stared at them. "You guys got tired? You're using your pods. You shouldn't get tired."

Greensleeves stretched and yawned. "I think it's one of the new things they added trying to make it more lifelike. I'll ask Rick about it when I get out of the pod for a while. I bet they don't have coffee here."

Baladara laughed. "You know there was a quest chain in one of the other games I played where I had to go a series of quests to gather beans, hot water, and something else for an NPC to make his own coffee, although he didn't call it that. I'd have to go back and check to see what it was." She frowned. "If I can even remember what game it was. That was a long time ago."

Greensleeves sighed. "I might have done that one too, back in high school. It sounds vaguely familiar."

Horc rolled his eyes. "I would think game designers would have better things to do with their time, and ours, than something like that." He reached for his leather armor he'd piled on the chair next to the bed.

"Hey, some of these strange little nonsense quests are the best ones," Baladara said. "They can be a real palate cleanser after some really tough ones where we have to battle our way through endless mobs to grind out some cash, or leather."

"Okay. Let's go grab some breakfast and get on the trail," Greensleeves said. "I'll send Steelmaiden a message to meet us downstairs."

"Sounds good." As Horc pulled on his boots, he realized something, a plus to the digital world. He hadn't had to hit the bathroom to relieve himself. He just hoped his pod was operating properly and taking care of those functions of his physical body the way it was supposed to.

Giving his wolf a quick head rub, Horc stood from his bed and waited for Greensleeves to finish getting dressed.

"You settled on getting a wolf companion." Baladara eyed the wolf. "Looks good. Are you going to name it, or just leave it as wolf?"

"I'd like to name it, but I haven't thought of a name yet." Horc patted the wolf again. "I've never had a pet before, so I'm not really sure what goes into naming them."

"You'll think of something," Greensleeves said. "That reminds me, I was going to show you how to put things in your quick launch bar so you don't have to go digging for them in the middle of a fight."

Baladara chuckled as they started out the door and down the stairs. "You're such a newb."

"Still learning the ropes," Horc said. "But I'm making progress. Greensleeves didn't need to tell me how to replace my equipment with something better yesterday. This new bow we got as a drop is great. Much faster than my original one."

"Wait till you get up a few more levels and start getting epic gear, then you'll know the meaning of fast and powerful." Baladara stopped at the foot of the stairs where they opened up to the main floor of the inn. There were only NPCs and Steelmaiden there. Without prompting, Baladara strode over to Steelmaiden. "Hi, I'm Baladara. Nice to have a tank in our group." She offered Steelmaiden her hand.

"Ah, you're the mage the boys told me about," Steelmaiden shook her hand, then gestured for them to join her at the table.

The NPC barmaid came over and took orders. Their fare was simple and limited, but was cheap enough, so Horc hoped it would be decent. He'd been really surprised that he could taste the stream water the previous day. He wasn't sure he wanted to encounter bad food in the game.

"Okay, let's get those quick launch bars of yours set up," Greensleeves said. "Do you mind if we take a look at your character sheet and see what we think you should have there?"

Although he wasn't sure how he'd feel with everyone looking at his character's raw stats but figured if he had issues then he might upset someone. He clicked on his character sheet and then hit the share button and shared it with all of them.

After a second, Baladara frowned. "Okay, wait a minute. You got access to your talent tree at level five and you haven't done anything with it. At this point you've got three points you can use to get talents."

Horc shrugged. "We've been busy most of the time and I wasn't exactly sure what to do with them."

"As a Ranger, you've got four different branches of the talent tree you can use," Steelmaiden said. "That's a lot for a Ranger. Have you thought about what you want to specialize in?"

"What's the benefits of specialization?" Horc asked, moving his arms off the table as the barmaid returned with their order.

"If you specialize in marksmanship, it looks like you get spells you can add to your arrows. Things like flaming arrows, explosive arrows, concussive arrows, DoT arrows, area of affect arrows." Steelmaiden read off the list of things.

"Wait a minute, dot arrows? What they leave marks on what you shoot? What benefit are those?"

Steelmaiden and Baladara both laughed and it took them a couple of moments to stop. Baladara was the first to recover. "Damage over time. Like poison. Your hit does the initial damage and then the next few rounds does a much lower amount of damage, but on targets that like to run off when they drop too far, that can be really handy."

"Okay. You say I've got three points I can use. What are the other specialties I can choose?"

Steelmaiden got herself under control and continued. "There's Companion specialties. It looks like you can do more with your companion, add to its attacks, or make it more robust. There's also Wildcrafting, that's things like snares, pit traps, tracking, and such. And lastly there's hand to hand skills, gives you extra bonuses and buffs on your axe attacks and also increases the number of weapons you can know."

"Wow, I'm going to need to think about that for a little while." Horc took a swig of the juice he'd ordered. It tasted just like orange juice. It even had a little bit of pulp in it.

"Okay, while you're thinking about that," Greensleeves said. "Let's look at the buffs and bonuses you already have that you aren't using." He tapped something on the character sheet and a window popped up. It was the same window Horc had used to find the Heal Companion spell the night before. "First, let's move your healing spell to the quick launch bar. If you'd tap on it twice."

Horc did as instructed and a drop-down menu appeared.

"Good. Select send to quick launch," Greensleeves instructed.

When Horc did that, a small square box appeared on the lower part of Horc's vision.

"I'm not sure in this game how many spells/abilities you can have on your quick launch," Greensleeves said. "Most games you can add things and delete them as you need to. So you can experiment with what feels right to you. You might also find that having certain things in particular locations works better. But if you look at this, you've got a few arrow spells you haven't been using. Here's a flaming one, and a multi shot one."

Horc blinked. "Wait, when did I get those spells? I haven't trained for them. This doesn't make sense. So far all I've gotten from Sureshot is quests."

"I wonder if it's happening when you're accepting your quests, or completing them," Baladara suggested.

"Some of the things need training and some don't," Steelmaiden said. "I've noticed with my own training some things like my sword attacks take training, and some things like my Battle Fury, I get automatically as I level up. Each class is going to be different, and without much in the wiki, we're not going to know how each one works for a while."

Horc spotted the attack spells Greensleeves mentioned and moved them to his quick launch. The flaming arrow spell did an additional 5 points of damage every second over three seconds. Also had a 5% chance to catch the target on fire to do 10 points more damage over 5 seconds and disrupt casters. It had a 6 second cooldown. The multi shot spell let him shoot two arrows at once at the same target. But had a 5 second cooldown. He couldn't wait to try them out.

"What more is there that I've missed?" Horc asked. He knew that everything he did helped him be better at the game and would improve his chances at staying alive.

"You've also got 5 stat points you haven't applied," Baladara said. "You're getting one of those every two levels."

Horc looked at his sheet. "Now I don't know what to do with those either. Part of me wants to dump them into constitution to give me more hit points, but that's just because I want to be harder to kill right now." He sighed. "But otherwise, I think I'd do something else."

"Do what you want to do," Greensleeves said. "You've got us to help keep you alive."

After the previous day, Horc knew he could rely on the three of them. With the new spells he'd be more dangerous. He was willing to take the chance. "Okay." He saw the spot where the stat points were and quickly added two points to his strength, one each to his intelligence, constitution, and stamina.

Greensleeves smiled and nodded. "Good choices."

"Oh, I just remembered that Lisa wanted me to tell you that the rescuers have put you low on the list for retrieval." Baladara leaned back in her chair. "Since we know you're alive and your pod is still functioning, they're going to focus on a few spots where there are more missing."

Horc nodded. "I'm good with that. Let them find the missing, although if I start slipping at least they know where I am." He didn't want to put other people in danger for his sake.

"Exactly." Baladara picked up a pastry. "So, Lisa said if she hears anything unusual, she'll interrupt and let me know."

"I just hope it doesn't happen in the middle of a fierce battle," Steelmaiden said.

"Got my fingers crossed." Baladara lifted her delicate hands showing her crossed digits, then licked the sugar from them.

"Good." Horc finished his eggs. "I guess I need to decide my specialty. I think it would be good to go with the Archer branch. It makes my distance attacks more dangerous. A Ranger is supposed to be a distance fighter, right. So, this is the logical choice." He opened up the Archer branch of the talent tree. The first level had three spells. An advancement of his fire arrow, it could have up to five points applied to it and did an additional 2 points of fire damage and an additional 5% chance to set the target on fire per point applied. There was an additional shot for his Multishot, it could get up to two points. There was also a targeting shot that would allow him to hit a target with a spell to make them easier to hit by 5% for him and his party for 5 seconds. It could handle up to three points with an additional 5% for each point although the time didn't go up.

After reviewing the spells, Horc dumped all three points into his flame arrow augment option. "Okay. I think I've got that taken care of."

Baladara put the last of her pastry in her mouth. "Good. I stopped by the mage trainer on the way to the inn to make sure there was nothing else I needed to learn. I'm still lower than you guys, but we should be able to take things out. Maybe if I'm lucky, I can level before we reach the dungeon."

"We can swing through some of the higher-level areas between here and there," Steelmaiden said. "No worries, we'll do what we can."

"Sounds good. Horc, did you get enough arrows before you went to bed?" Baladara asked.

Horc shook his head. "I still need to sell a bunch of the loot we got, too."

"Then let's stop by a weaponsmith on our way out of town." Steelmaiden stood, then threw back the last of her juice.

Horc opened his bag to get a chunk of meat. He tossed it to the wolf. He felt better about heading into the dungeon with Baladara along for the fight and with his updated fighting skills. He was having enough fun in the game that he didn't want to stop and he didn't want to worry about dying. With his party, he wasn't going to have to worry about that.

16

BY THE time they reached the Gnoll King's Dungeon, Baladara had managed to get up to level eight. She was happy and ready to kick some Gnoll tail. Horc was nearly to level eleven. He wished he'd gotten a few more XP to be able to level, but he figured he'd get them fairly soon after entering the dungeon. They'd stopped by the quest-givers in the encampment and took all the quests they could that had anything to do with the dungeon.

Baladara paused just before the opening to the cave that led to the dungeon. "Horc, take these." She opened up a trade window and there were twenty health potions in there.

Horc looked at the window. "Are you sure I need them? We've got Greensleeves to help if my health starts dropping."

She nodded. "Look, we might have times when his mana is too low to cast a healing spell, or he might be busy with another spell and can't get to you in time. They aren't great, powerful healing potions, but they were all I could make with my potions skill. They should be enough to keep you alive until Greensleeves can get to you, or until we get out of battle. They have a 30 second non-combat cooldown and get you between 200 and 300 health. Now take them."

He accepted the trade and the potions popped into his bag. Horc didn't like the idea of being so dependent on his friends and party mates, but it was better than sitting around in the inn all day.

"She's got a good point," Greensleeves said. "This is also a good time to put some buffs on everyone. Baladara and I both have some useful buffs that will make this a lot easier for everyone. Let me start." His hands blurred and seconds later a dark brown glow surrounded Horc. Then he did another spell and a red glow encompassed Horc. "This first spell was a Briar Shield. For one hour it causes one point of damage when attacked and gives two percent chance of vines entangling attacker to slow them down for five seconds. The second spell was an Animal Deflection spell. For thirty minutes any animal attack will be lessened by twenty five percent. Unfortunately, it doesn't affect poisons."

Horc grinned. "Hey, any little bit helps. Do we expect to run into animals in a dungeon?"

Greensleeves shrugged as he turned to cast the buffs on Steelmaiden. "You never actually know. Just about anything can be in a dungeon in some games."

"He's right." Baladara rubbed her hands together. "Okay. I've only got one spell that will be useful, and you're all going to have to keep track of what I cast on you; things might get busy and I don't want people dying when my spell could've helped." She moved her hands and a scintillating silver glow covered Horc. "This is an Arcane Shield. It lasts for 10 minutes and cuts attack blows by twenty five percent. It's one that helps mages have nearly the same armor as people in leather armor."

"Sweet." Horc glanced around and noticed three small icons right above his quick launch bar. He tapped them and could see where they were all doing countdowns. Each one opened and had a brief summary similar to what Baladara and Greensleeves had said.

When the two casters finished distributing their buffs, they both sat down and drank. Before the drinking, Greensleeves's mana had dropped to almost a quarter and

Baladara's was just over a half. When they were finished, they were ready.

Steelmaiden pulled her massive sword. "Let's do this." She stalked into the cave.

The moment Horc entered the cave, he felt disoriented and he suddenly wanted to throw up. The feeling passed and they were somewhere else. Where the cave had been flat, there was suddenly a passage sloping down.

"Alright, what just happened?" Horc looked around. The rest of the party looked a little green in the gills too.

"Wow." Baladara shook her head. "That has got to be the worst dungeon server jump I have ever felt."

Horc frowned. "Dungeon server jump? What does that even mean?"

Greensleeves leaned on his staff. "Each dungeon is on its own server. Rick said they'd thought about trying to let a single AI handle the base game and the dungeons too, but it got to be too much. A lot of fantasy games do it this way to help minimize server lag when there's a ton of players online. But yeah, it shouldn't have been that bad."

"That's definitely going into my beta report," Steelmaiden grumbled. "Okay. I don't want to do that anymore than I have to, so let's see what we can do about kicking this dungeon's ass in one try."

"Sounds good to me," Horc agreed. "Now I guess we need to find the monsters. With the quests I've got there's a lot of different things that need killing."

"Right." Steelmaiden started off down the passageway without another word.

The passageway continued down for a good distance. When it grew dark, Baladara cast a light spell.

"Okay, this is going to suck if I have to keep the light spell going the whole way," Baladara grumbled as they trudged along. "What do parties without a Mage or Witch do for light?"

"Ask their Paladin to do something holy." Greensleeves said with a soft chuckle.

"Or maybe their Barbarian knows how to make a torch," Steelmaiden said.

"Then why didn't ours, before I had to cast light?" Baladara quipped.

"Because ours wants to keep her big sword in hand at all times for when we start running into monsters."

As the words left her mouth, a huge spider jumped out into the middle of the passage. It was easily as big as Horc's wolf. Steelmaiden hit it first, her large sword swinging fast and sharp.

Spider guts splattered the wall as Horc got a lock on it. **Cave Webwalker level 12**. Its health was beginning to fall as Horc backed up and started firing arrows at it. As he'd practiced on the way to the dungeon, he started with a Multishot Barrage, and followed up with a Flame Arrow. When he needed to give the spells time to cooldown, he continued firing regular arrows as fast as he could. Wolf had rushed up to help Steelmaiden in close combat as Greensleeves and Baladara stood at Horc's side slinging spells. Within moments, the spider was down.

Steelmaiden handled the loot while the others stood ready should another appear.

"Okay. I know it's the first monster in the dungeon, but I guess I was hoping for more," she grumbled as she straightened and a few coppers clinked into Horc's bag.

"Like those guys?" Greensleeves asked as three more spiders entered the area covered by Baladara's light.

"Yeah!" Steelmaiden shouted and threw herself into the fray.

Horc repeated his firing sequence and the spider he targeted bypassed Steelmaiden and his wolf to head right toward him. It was a level 13. He hit it as hard and fast as he could while the others engaged the rest of the monsters. It still had half its level when it reached Horc and hit him with a web attack. That cut his movement, but since it didn't reach his arms, he dropped his bow and yanked out his axe. The spider's first direct hit knocked a good chunk out of his health. Horc hit it as hard as he could. He chopped off one of its legs in a single blow.

The spider hissed at him and bit him in the leg. Another chunk of his health dropped and he was down to three quarters. Nothing to really worry about, as long as he or Greensleeves got things under control quickly.

His wolf broke off its attack on the spider Steelmaiden was fighting and rushed to Horc's aid. Together they got it taken care of before it could take him down to under a quarter.

Greensleeves and Baladara were still fighting their spider, although its health bar was flashing orange.

Horc targeted the beast Steelmaiden was battling as he picked up his bow and fired a Multishot attack as fast as he could. His wolf followed the arrows down the passageway, and when it struck at the same time as Steelmaiden, the spider shook and dropped.

Swinging his bow toward the spider the two casters were fighting, Horc got a single Flaming Arrow off before it stopped moving and fell over.

"Okay, I don't understand why they didn't all aggro on me," Steelmaiden said as she bent over to loot her spider.

Horc looted his.

"Did you hit them first?" Greensleeves asked as Baladara looted their spider.

Steelmaiden paused and looked thoughtful as she ran a hand through her long red hair. "I don't think so, there wasn't time. Oh, and I forgot to do my War Cry. Next time there's more than one of them, I'll do that and it'll make all the attackers within my area of effect come at me, so you guys can pick them off without a problem."

As he finished looting the spider, Horc sat and pulled out a ration bar and a skin of water. "Hey, I'm glad I'm not the only one stumbling from time to time. We'll all get it down."

Baladara took a seat next to him. "You got that right. You're clicking in with the arrow spells pretty fast though."

Horc glowed a bit under the praise. He wanted to do well. Having the others with him in the game helped, but it was nice pulling his own weight in the party. He tossed the spider leg he'd just gotten in loot to the wolf. It happily crunched it until it was all gone.

"Hey, I think it's getting lighter up ahead," Steelmaiden said as the spiders around them vanished. "Let's keep moving."

Since his health and mana bars were back to full, Horc rose, then offered Baladara a hand up. They'd just started the dungeon and none of them knew how long it was going to take.

17

HORC LEANED against the wall and panted. They never seemed to get all the way to the light. It seemed to retreat farther and farther from them, and at the same time more and more monsters jumped out at them from every twist and turn in the passageway.

They barely had time to defeat one batch of spiders before giant grubs were on them, then there were more spiders. So far, they hadn't encountered a single Gnoll; it was supposed to be a Gnoll dungeon.

"This has all got to be the first level of this dungeon," Steelmaiden said as she wiped spider gore off her sword. "I hope it will improve with the second level."

"I'm guessing we don't know how many levels there are to this dungeon," Horc said.

"There was an update in the wiki for this instance," Baladara said. "I checked it this morning before logging in. There are five levels and we will encounter Gnolls before the end. People are complaining that the dungeon is really hard for the suggested levels. A lot of people are saying they're avoiding it until they're at least level fifteen."

Steelmaiden huffed. "They don't like a real challenge. They were looking for a stroll down to the pub since the game is still in beta at the moment. Let's keep going and show them how a dungeon is done."

"With lots of screaming and gore flying in all directions?" Horc asked with a smirk. He wasn't sure what to make of the way Steelmaiden screamed her War Cry each time they encountered more than one opponent.

It was nice though, that all the gore they splattered across the passageway and each other disappeared after a couple of minutes.

"Keeps the bad guys off you all so you can do your damage while I take the hits." Steelmaiden grinned. "That's what a tank is supposed to do."

Holding her sword high, she started walking on down the passageway. "Now let's clear out this level and get on to more interesting stuff."

With quick nods they fell in behind her with Horc's wolf pacing more at her side than Horc's. It didn't really bother him because the wolf always went after whichever attacker Horc fired on, whether it was the one Steelmaiden had engaged or not.

They made it around two twists in the passageway before the next attack. Five spiders rushed them. They ranged in level from eleven to fourteen.

Steelmaiden shouted at the top of her lungs. Her War Cry rang out through the passageway. The spiders that had been rushing past her turned and attacked.

Horc fired as fast as he could. Making sure to use DoT attacks first so he could move on to another target and have them all getting damage as the battle raged. He nearly cheered when one of them burst into flames. It was the first time he'd gotten the flame bonus effect. The spider hissed but kept attacking Steelmaiden as it burned. For good measure, Horc shot it several more times before moving on to the next one. His wolf was attacking whichever one he'd just shot, so it moved around quickly, but the spiders were so focused on Steelmaiden they didn't seem to care.

Every time her health dropped too low, the blue aura of Greensleeves's healing spell appeared around Steelmaiden, normally just after he'd hit something with a blazing green Druid attack spell.

One spider went down and it was easier for Horc to do more damage to the others.

"How dare you intrude on my territory!" a deep voice bellowed from the darkness.

Horc looked around as he pulled more arrows for another Multishot attack. There wasn't anything more than the spiders in the light, although the voice sounded like it had come from the same direction as the arachnids.

As the second spider fell, huge multi-jointed legs came into the light.

"Ah, crap," Baladara said from beside Horc. "We need to finish these spiders off quick."

"What is it?" Horc asked. He tried targeting it but couldn't get either a lock or an ID on the creature.

"Big." Baladara got off a fireball that ended the third spider.

As they continued to attack the spiders, the body of a huge arachnid eased its way into the light. It seemed to be moving almost too slowly. The body that emerged didn't look right either, but Horc wasn't sure what it was that looked wrong about it.

With every shot, he glanced back at the thing coming toward them as the shadows slipped farther away for it. The fourth spider fell to Steelmaiden and she tilted her head back as if to use her War Cry, but no sound came out.

The thing that had been moving slowly, suddenly rushed forward. The rest of it entered the light all in one fell swoop. It wasn't a spider at all, but some kind of weird spider-human hybrid. Its bulbous body was smooth like a black widow spider, but the human torso was hairy like a gorilla, even if it did seem to have human-sized breasts. Its head was bald with piercing red eyes and thin lips. When Horc could get a weapons lock on it, the deep red text above its human head said **Dolowitz Webwalker**

Herder, level 16. And there were two stars next to the name.

It slashed at Steelmaiden with a long spear. It knocked half of the health Greensleeves had just regenerated in her. She screamed. It was a much different sound than her battle cries. There was an edge of pain to it Horc had never heard from her before.

"I've got you!" Greensleeves shouted as he started his healing spells.

"Together!" Baladara yelled as she cast her first fireball at the monster.

Horc didn't need to be told twice. They hadn't taken on a monster of this level before, let alone one that had two stars beside its name. He used Multishot, followed by a Flaming Arrow. Wolf jumped on it from behind. Even after Baladara's fireball hit, its health bar barely budged.

Everything fell away as Horc focused his attacks on the herder. It was big and nasty as it went after Baladara. She was casting spells as fast as she could, her mana dropping as each spell left her fingers. Since the thing was giving her all his attention, Horc was able to keep his distance and keep firing his arrows. The Fire Arrows seemed to help little by little, but Horc noticed that his mana was starting down too, just not as fast.

Wolf yelped as the herder flung it to the side and it hit the passageway wall. It landed on its feet and rushed back in. Thankfully, its health wasn't majorly impacted by the attack.

Then Steelmaiden jumped on it from behind, driving her massive sword deep into the thing's thorax. The herder screamed and smashed her in the side of her head with his spear. She lost a grip on her sword and went flying off. She'd lost half of her health again, and the monster was down only a quarter.

Steelmaiden shouted something and a huge ghostly wolf appeared at her side, then rushed into battle.

Horc's mind reeled as he continued to sling arrows at it. They'd been pounding on it with all they had and had barely made a dent in it. What was it going to take to stop the thing?

Vines rose up out of the floor and wrapped around the herder's legs. It struggled in their grasp, turning its spear to the task of trying to free itself. While it was distracted, Baladara pulled out a potion and quickly downed it. Her health went up a bit, but not a lot. The wolf Steelmaiden summoned slashed at it frantically, moving faster than Horc's companion wolf did.

Horc fired another barrage of Multishot and Flaming Arrows. The herder caught fire. The vines caught fire as well. The herder struggled harder as its health bar dropped more, but there was still more than half its health left.

Baladara's next fire ball seemed to do more damage.

Horc fired regular arrows as he wished the cooldown on his Flame Arrows would hurry up and finish. The second they were ready, he cast the spell again. His mana was down to about a quarter. Without the spell bonuses from the special arrows, he wasn't sure how they were going to defeat the herder.

The vines retreated into the floor, leaving smudges on the stone where they passed. The herder charged Greensleeves. The Druid swung his staff as he finished healing Steelmaiden.

She jumped back onto the herder and hacked at it with her sword. Horc's Flame Arrow cooldown ended and he got another arrow off, then continued to fire as fast as he could. His fingers began to ache.

With his next fire spell, his mana flashed red.

The spectral wolf vanished.

"Die, you ugly bug!" Baladara shouted and rushed the herder, swinging her short sword as she went. Wondering why she was engaging it in close combat, Horc glanced at her mana bar, it was empty. His own was getting close to that, but even if it happened, he could still shoot arrows; they just wouldn't be special.

The herder swung his spear in a huge arc. It knocked Steelmaiden and Horc's wolf back. Somehow Baladara managed to stop it with her staff, but she shook with the effort and her health dropped again.

Horc took a deep breath and carefully aimed his next arrow as his fire arrow became available again. The shot took the monster in the eye and caught fire again. The thing screamed and tore at its face to yank the arrow out.

Greensleeves's vines stopped it again, as Steelmaiden roared and threw herself at it. Her avatar in the party list flashed bright orange and continued to pulse as she hacked at the herder.

"All together!" Greensleeves shouted as the herder's health dropped to below a quarter.

Horc fired arrow after arrow as Greensleeves hit the thing with several bolts of Druid magic. Baladara managed to get another Fireball off, then her mana bar was empty again. She slashed at the thing's legs with her sword and Horc's wolf at her side.

When Horc's Flame Arrow spell didn't come back as fast as he thought it should, he glanced at his mana. It was empty. With a frown, he kept firing. That was all he could do. If the monster got too close, he'd have to switch to his axe and do as much damage as he could. Then, suddenly the battle was over. The herder dropped to the ground. Steelmaiden raised her sword into the air and screamed at the top of her lungs. Her avatar stopped flashing and she dropped to her knees.

The gold leveling aura shot around Horc. **Level 11**

Similar auras flashed around Greensleeves and Steelmaiden. Baladara was the only one who didn't level due to the monster's death.

"Everyone eat and drink," Greensleeves urged. "We've got to be ready in case there are more of those."

Horc's health was fine, and his mana was full. "Hey, we just leveled. I don't think we need to eat and drink." He studied the downed monster. "Is it just me, or does this thing's head look like Johan Dolowitz, our office director?"

"Speak for yourself," Baladara snapped. "I almost leveled, but barely missed it. That thing was nasty." She paused like she was just processing the last bit of what he'd said, then she stared at the herder. "Damn, you're right. That nasty thing does look like Mr. Dolowitz. Oh my god. You've got to be kidding me. The game designers modeled the bosses after real bosses." She burst out laughing.

"Do we think it *was* the boss for this level of the dungeon?" Steelmaiden started looting the herder.

Horc turned to looting the spiders. Coins clinked into everyone's pockets.

"I don't know," Greensleeves said. "Since most of the monsters we've encountered didn't have two stars, it could be. Or maybe there's something bigger down the cave. I think I can definitely see the designers having a warped enough sense of humor to model the bosses after people in the company. They're probably figuring they'll never play and don't have to worry about getting in trouble."

Horc wasn't sure he wanted to see anything bigger than that until they had a few more levels.

"Wahooo!" Steelmaiden hefted the things spear into the air. "I don't think any of the rest of you can use a spear, can you?"

"Not me," Greensleeves and Baladara said at the same time.

"I don't think so," Horc said, unsure of how to tell if he could use it or not.

"This is better than my sword." She waved the spear around. "I'm keeping it." She pulled the sword from her back and slipped it into her pack, then she slipped the spear onto her back. "Yeah, this is nice. Dungeons are great for awesome gear and this spear is great. Perfect for my level too."

"Anything else great on this one?" Baladara put her water skin back in her bag.

Steelmaiden rifled through the corpse. "Some spider meat and…oh, wait…quest item. We all got the quest for the herder's spinnerets, didn't we?"

Horc nearly cried as he checked his quest log and there was the quest of **The Herder's Spinnerets**. "Does this mean we've got to wait for this thing to respawn and kill it three more times?" He wasn't sure any of them would survive the dungeon if, for each special item they were supposed to bring back, they had to kill the monster four times.

"Dungeons often operate differently than the regular part of the game," Baladara said as she walked over to the corpse. "First, things don't normally respawn unless you leave the dungeon and come back in, often after a server reset." She knelt at the herder and pulled something out. "Yep, we should all be able to get the quest items."

The news made Horc relax. He went to the herder and found the spinnerets he needed and a message flashed on his screen.

The Herder's Spinnerets quest complete

There was also a blue egg-shaped crystal there. He grabbed both and put them in his bag.

The rest of the spiders were just worth some coins, spider meat and broken legs. At least Horc wasn't going to have trouble feeding his wolf in the dungeon. With all the spider meat they'd accumulated, along with the bear, boar, and wolf meat from the farming they'd done on the dungeon, he was set pretty well.

Once they had all recovered from the fight, they continued down the passage. They hit a few more spiders as they worked their way lower and lower. When they encountered a heavy wooden door, they paused.

"No more big nasties," Baladara said. "What do you guys think? Is this the end of this level, or is the boss for this level behind this door?"

Greensleeves shrugged. "I guess we won't know until we open the door and find out."

"I was afraid you were going to say that." Horc nocked an arrow and stepped back. "Steelmaiden, if you would do the honors of opening the door."

The big barbarian gripped her new spear as she pulled on the door's wooden handle. Horc hoped if there was anything on the other side of the door, they'd be taking it by surprise.

Steelmaiden frowned, then pushed on the door. "I think it's locked. But the knob turns."

Baladara walked up to it. "That doesn't make any sense." She put her hand on the door. "It doesn't feel like there's any innate magic in it." She paused and traced an indention in the door. "I wonder if this is some kind of key hole."

"What do you mean?" Steelmaiden leaned closer to the door, looking at the spot. "Well it doesn't look natural. Looks almost like an egg would go in there."

"An egg?" Horc asked, then touched his bag. "Wait a minute." He slung his bow over his shoulder and reached in his bag and pulled out the blue egg-shaped crystal he'd found when he'd found the spinnerets. "Like this?"

Baladara took the crystal from him. "Let's see. Where did you find it?"

"On the boss." Horc fought the urge to ask to be the one to try the crystal in the door, but if it blew up, she had a better chance of surviving in real life than he did.

As if she had heard his thoughts, Baladara handed the crystal to Steelmaiden. "You're our tank. See what happens."

"Okay." Steelmaiden took the crystal and put it into the spot on the door.

The door flashed a brilliant blue, the same color as the crystal, then it cracked open slightly.

Steelmaiden pulled the crystal out of the door and handed it back to Horc. "Keep it in case we need it for the next door."

"Will do." Horc slipped it into his bag with a nod. The flash had been so bright that he really hoped it hadn't alerted anything on the other side to their impending arrival. While Steelmaiden finished opening the door, he held his breath as he pulled his bow and prepared for whatever was about to attack them.

18

THE DOOR creaked open. Horc was pretty sure they were all holding their breath. Light spilled out from beyond the door. Nothing else happened. Steelmaiden hefted her spear and went on through the door.

She sighed. "Looks like we're going on down from here."

"You know, it would be nice if these dungeons would come with sign posts, or something that told us the first level is over and we're starting the second," Baladara said.

"Asking for a lot there, aren't you?" Greensleeves said as he held the door for Horc and his wolf to pass. "Maybe they can put some kind of notice on the door. I'll mention it to Rick, but I bet he's going to laugh his head off."

"Probably," Steelmaiden said.

The slowly sloping passage turned into a series of stairs.

"Any idea where the light is coming from?" Horc asked as they descended the stone steps. It was nearly daytime bright but he didn't see any obvious source of the illumination. He glanced down for shadows, but he couldn't spot any in any direction.

"Magic," Baladara said. "It's the only thing that makes sense. So, let's not have any kind of magic cancelling spells for a while. I'm tired of casting the light spell. I might be able to get off a few extra Fireballs if I don't have to devote mana to that."

"We'll do what we can," Horc said. It made sense to keep from killing the lights. He liked moving through the well-illuminated space as opposed to struggling to pierce the darkness beyond the glow from Baladara's spells.

They walked down the stairs for what felt like forever. Nothing changed as they went. It was stair after stair. The air was still and musty, feeling as if there hadn't been a breeze of any sort in many years. Their steps rang out with each step. As loud as they were, Horc wondered what kind of cacophony would've erupted if one of them had been in plate mail.

"How long is this going to last?" Greensleeves muttered from behind Horc.

"No clue," Baladara replied. "At least we haven't hit any…"

Steelmaiden slammed the butt of her spear into Baladara's foot. "Don't say anything like that. It'll bring bad luck."

"Hey!" Baladara reached down and rubbed her foot. "You didn't need to do that."

With a grin and a shrug, Steelmaiden continued down the stairs. "But it got you to shut up."

For some reason, her actions and tones reminded Horc of how his mother would stomp on either his foot or his father's when she wanted to distract them. As they walked, he realized they didn't even know her real name. They knew she was from the Dublin office, and that she was using a pod, but that was it.

Before Horc could bring himself to ask her any questions, Steelmaiden roared and charged off the stairs onto a flat even floor that looked like marble tile. He and the others hurried down the last couple of steps onto the floor. The room they entered looked like an old Greek temple. There were massive stone pillars that went from the marble floor up to the rough rock ceiling.

Ahead of them, Steelmaiden was battling a huge serpent woman who had the lower body of a snake and the upper torso of a woman with a mass of writhing green hair. The text, when Horc targeted her, said **Gorgon Priestess, level 13.** He was thankful there weren't any stars next to her name. He fired a Multishot Barrage and wolf leapt into action as Greensleeves and Baladara got off their spells.

The snakes that made up the Gorgon's lashed out like whips, striking Steelmaiden on the arms as she batted at them with her spear. As each snake stopped moving the Gorgon's health dropped.

"Aim for the snakes of her hair!" Horc shouted as he focused his aim on the writhing green hair. Although while focusing, he couldn't target two snakes with his Multishot attack, his Flame Arrow did its job. When he wasn't able to cast fire, it took two shots to take out a snake head.

"Look out, she's casting!" Steelmaiden shouted and hit the Gorgon's hands with her spear. The move gave the snakes more opportunity to strike, but it stopped the Gorgon from casting.

"Hang on, I'll counter the poison." Greensleeves cast his own spell.

Baladara got off a Fireball and managed to set the monster's hair on fire. The snake woman screamed and tried to shove away from Steelmaiden, but Horc's wolf was on the back of its tail biting hard, preventing it from completely turning around.

Horc continued to shoot arrows into its serpentine tresses. By the time they all stopped moving, the monster was down to a little over a quarter of her health and she was trying desperately to get away, making it hard for Steelmaiden and the wolf to keep her in place so Horc and the casters could continue to blast her.

Finally, she straightened to her full height, throwing Steelmaiden and the wolf off, screamed and fell to the marble floor dead.

The golden glow of leveling hit Baladara. "Yes, about damn time. I made level nine."

"Good, now let's loot, get stats back where they should be and keep moving," Steelmaiden said. "I've got a feeling I'm not going to like this level."

"Got issues with snakes?" Baladara asked as she sat to have a drink.

"I'm Irish," Steelmaiden snapped as she finished looting the corpse. "Of course I have an issue with snakes."

A hefty clink of coins came from everyone's pouches.

"You realize that the snakes Saint Patrick got rid of weren't real snakes but druids, don't' you?" Greensleeves asked as he settled next to Baladara.

Steelmaiden rolled her eyes. "Of course I do. But I still don't like serpents of any kind. They're creepy in their leglessness."

"Then you have an issue with worms too?" Horc tossed a chunk of meat to the wolf. "You didn't react badly with the grubs earlier."

"Those are a little different. They weren't as…predatory." Steelmaiden shrugged as if at a loss for words.

"We'll just accept your phobia and go on," Baladara said. "But the grubs were trying to kill us, just like everything else in this vicious hole in the ground."

They were all back up to max health and mana, and together, they stood and stared around the temple.

"I wonder what else is around here," Greensleeves asked as he walked farther into the room. "Although the spiders weren't all bunched up, they were there every little bit. It makes sense there would be more to this area than just the one snake lady."

"Okay, just be careful." Horc nocked an arrow and followed Greensleeves with his wolf at his side.

"Hey"—Steelmaiden stomped in front of them—"I'm the tank. I take point."

"She's got the big spear," Baladara said. "Let her take *point*."

"Sure, no problem." Greensleeves stopped and let Steelmaiden step in front of him, just in time for another of the Gorgons to slither out and attack them.

Knowing the snake woman's general weakness, Horc focused his attacks on the monster's hair until every snake was dead and she was at half healthy, then he hit her with his standard combo as the rest of the team did their jobs. They offed the second Gorgon faster than they had the first.

They worked on through the dungeon, killing Gorgons and giant snakes as they went. Each new type caused them to stumble a little in how quickly they could take things out, but once they had a monster's weakness, it was a fairly simple job to exploit that flaw in their armor and bring them down.

The Gorgons seemed to be the monster of the level as they worked their way through the underground temple. They were more populous than the giant snakes and seemed to grow more powerful the farther they went into the level.

As they stopped after killing their latest opponent, a level seventeen Gorgon warrior, Horc asked. "Is the whole dungeon going to be this way?"

Steelmaiden frowned. "What way?"

"Every step we take just brings us in conflict with stronger and stronger monsters. How are we going to survive this? It's getting to be harder and harder."

"But these higher level beasties give us more XP," Baladara said. "I'm about to level again, and that's good."

Horc checked his XP bar, and sure enough he was about to level too. He had to admit that even with the party split, getting 100 to 150 XP per monster was helping him a lot. They were also giving a decent amount of coins per drop. If he was able to do the dungeon without help, he would've been making bank on it, but he wasn't going to complain the way it was going.

Something clanged on the marble floor and all of them jerked to their feet and brought their weapons to ready.

A big man in heavy armor ran into the temple. His heavy metal boots rang out with each step. The text above his head read **Slasher, Human, Warrior, level 12**. He stopped and stared their direction. "Dudes, this dungeon is a complete pain in the ass."

"Are you here by yourself?" Steelmaiden asked. "In the middle of a dungeon? It's one thing to run a dungeon solo when you're twenty or thirty levels above it, but at the same level, that's nuts."

Slasher pulled off his helm and rubbed his face. "Look. I'm not nuts. I came in here with four friends. We figured with five of us, two were healers, me to tank and two DPS, we should be able to do it. We all died several times in the first level, our healers ducked out, claiming they needed to go to bed. When the Witch and the Mage got killed, they didn't come back in. Luckily I've got some potions and found this awesome spear." He held up the same spear Steelmaiden had looted from the first level boss. "But I've been working my way out of here. I figure I'll wait until my friends get a few more levels and try again."

Baladara put her hands on her hips and shook her head. "Friends don't leave friends to die in dungeons.

Look, we could use another good tank. We have an awesome one right now, but like you guys, we didn't expect the dungeon to kick us around the way it has. You want to finish it with us?"

"Sure, why not?" Slasher looked past them, back toward the door they'd come through that would lead back to the first level. "That'll show them what happens when you leave friends behind."

Steelmaiden nodded. "Right. Now, before we go too far, I've got a question for you. First, what office are you out of?"

"I'm Theo Davenport, operations manager in the Long Beach office." Slasher offered her his hand.

Horc was a little surprised to find someone else from management in there, especially upper management. Slasher shouldn't have needed the extra cash for the beta run.

"Marianne McGuffin, supply line, Dublin office." She returned his handshake.

Slasher turned to Greensleeves.

"I'm David Remington, hiring agent in the Atlanta office. My husband is Rick Remington, one of the game designers."

Slasher's mouth dropped open. "Wait a minute. We've got an alert on you and your party a few hours ago." He looked at Horc. "That mean you must be Alan Gosling from the Dallas office, the guy trapped in his pod. Dude, we're all supposed to be on the lookout for you. You're on a do-not-kill list. Any player caught killing you will be termed and if you die IRL because of it, they will be brought up on charges. Wow. Yeah. I'll help keep you alive."

Horc wasn't sure what to say. He didn't want people hanging around just to try to keep him alive, and he had no idea the company had put out a do-not-kill list among the employees. "Thanks for lending a hand," Horc finally said as Slasher shook his hand. "I wonder if that alert went out while we were sleeping."

"Dude, we're all amazed a natural disaster strikes the same night we launch out beta for Halfworld." Slasher shook his head. "I mean, what are the odds?"

"Oh," Baladara pushed her way next to Horc. "I'm Mike Simmons IRL, also from the Dallas office. Tech support." He looked a little confused. "You know, I didn't see any alert on our party, but I wonder."

"Nice to meet you, Mike." Slasher shook his hand too. "Well, cool then. Let's keep this show on the road. If you guys could just invite me to the party, we'll groove along."

"Sure, why not?" Baladara sounded a bit bitchy, but seconds later, Slasher's avatar joined the list on the right side of Horc's vision. The Baladara got a faraway look. "Oh, okay. Yeah there was a system wide alter put out on us. It helps to read all the alerts that go out."

"Sure does," Horc agreed, then felt a little silly about not knowing about the alert either, or worse, how to check for system alters. He'd wait until they got out of the dungeon before asking anyone about that. "So, let's keep pounding away at this level."

"Definitely," Greensleeves said. "Now that we've got two tanks, I'll do my best to keep perma-locks on both of you to make it easier to heal you, although the split-screen interface might get a little confusing. Oh, Slasher, are you helmet and gloves, or Pod?"

"Pod. My wife hates it, but since I've promised her a new hot tub with the beta money, she agreed to let me get it. I can't believe it took me years to get a pod when I've been working for the company that's developed most of the tech for them." Slasher put his helm back in place. "But hey, at least when I'm in the pod, my wife knows where I am, not like when I'm surfing." He laughed.

Steelmaiden glared for a second, then turned toward the far end of the temple. "Okay, since you've been through part of this, I'll let you lead."

Slasher stepped in front of her. "Cool. Yeah. I've been doing my best not to aggro some of the meaner stuff. My party was doing pretty good at that too."

"Then how did they get killed if they were trying to not aggro things?" Steelmaiden shook her head. "You're in upper management, were all of your friends too?"

"What happens in game stays in game, right?" Slasher sounded a little skeptical.

Steelmaiden grinned, as did Baladara.

"We're all here to just have a little fun," Greensleeves said before either one of them could utter a word.

"And stay alive," Horc added. "Staying alive is very important right now." He didn't really care if Slasher's friends were management or not, but if they were, it would explain why they were so quick to run out on him when the going got rough. He'd learned a long time ago that most corporate management were just out for themselves. They'd get what they could out of a company and then run off to the next big thing they could destroy. A game like Halfworld would be perfect for them. They could loot to their hearts' content and not have to worry about the consequences.

Slasher raised his spear high. "Here's to everyone staying alive."

Steelmaiden also raised her spear but didn't say anything. They all followed Slasher deeper into the dungeon and Horc hoped again that they weren't all in over their heads.

19

THE FIRST three monsters they encountered with Slasher along were more of the Gorgons. Since they had a pattern down, his help sped up the process, and they went down smoothly. But it was only the second level of the dungeon; there were a lot of things that could go wrong, too many possibilities for trouble.

Two massive cobras, both longer than any of the party were tall, slithered toward them. When Horc targeted the first one, the red text read **Sacred Temple Cobra, level 18.** His heart skipped a beat. They hadn't taken on anything like that yet, and there were two of them.

"Horc, go for the one on the right," Baladara said as her hands danced in the start of her spell. "Cover Steelmaiden."

Horc nodded and as Steelmaiden screamed her War Cry, drawing the cobra's attention, he unleashed his first round of Multishot. The arrows slammed into the snake as Baladara rammed her spear into it. The cobra rose up high, pulling the Barbarian off her feet. She kicked it hard as Horc's wolf connected with the serpent and started pulling out huge chunks.

The second snake had stopped a short distance back and started a strange whistling noise. Slasher paused and stared at it, appearing unable to move.

Baladara's spell hit it hard, but it didn't seem to react.

"Crap," Greensleeves shouted. "It's got him hypnotized. Horc, change targets. Aim for its neck, let's see if we can interrupt that whistle."

Not needing to be told twice, Horc switched his weapon's lock to the one entrancing Slasher. His first Flame Arrow made it jerk back, but it continued casting its spell. He pulled another arrow back, waiting for the cooldown time to finish so he could hit harder, then hit it with Multishot, followed closely by another Flame Arrow and a regular arrow.

Although he was managing to do a little bit of damage with each arrow, he hadn't broken the thing's spell yet. Slasher stood there a few feet from it, like he was waiting for it to kill him. Horc took a deep breath and focused hard on the snake's lips, that scaly perfect circle where the sound was coming out. He unleashed his arrow and it flew into the cobra's mouth. The thing's song stopped and it jerked its head up. The shot had criticaled and cost it half of its health.

Horc's wolf had changed targets, going after the one Horc was firing on. It hit the cobra hard, knocking it back as Slasher shook his head, coming out of the trance.

With a wild "Wahoo!", Slasher stabbed the cobra with his spear. He planted his feet and pushed as Horc unleashed another Multishot volley followed by a Flame Arrow. The Flame Arrow caught the cobra on fire. Its health dropped to a little under a quarter and began to flash orange.

"Die!" Slasher yelled and yanked his spear out of the cobra to jam it up into the thing's jaws as hard as he could.

Horc managed to get another Flaming Arrow into the thing's eye. Its health flashed red, and with the last snap of the wolf's jaws, it fell to the floor.

"A little help here, guys!" Steelmaiden shouted. Her cobra wasn't even half down and her health bar was fading as the thing bit her in the shoulder and lifted her up. Her spectral wolf was fading away.

Greensleeves' healing spell wrapped her in blue for a second, as Horc switched targets and got off a Flame Arrow before the cooldown on his Multishot finished. Then he unleashed a volley of arrows at it, followed by a single shot.

The cobra dropped Steelmaiden and stared right at Horc.

A bolt of fear went through him. The creature still had nearly half of its health and looked like it was coming for him. Slasher jumped in front of Horc and thrust his spear into the thing's chest. The cobra spat venom at him. Slasher yanked out his spear and tore off his helm. His face was smoking.

Horc's wolf made it back to that cobra and bit it in the side, his claws ripping scales off as he held on tightly. Greensleeves's hands glowed as he continued getting spells off trying to heal Slasher and Steelmaiden.

As Horc continued to pepper the thing with arrows, Steelmaiden jabbed her spear repeatedly in the thing's chest and abdomen. She drove her spear up into its jaws, effectively stopping it from being able to spit.

"Your spear!" She shouted as she ran toward Slasher who was still wiping his face even as Greensleeves cast another round of healing, this one with the purple hue Horc recognized as an Anti-poison spell.

He tossed her the spear.

Horc got off more arrows. The cobra burst into flames. Steelmaiden rammed Slasher's spear hard into the cobra. Its health flashed orange. Horc hit it with another Multishot as his wolf tore more chunks out of it. The cobra shuddered and went down.

Greensleeves hurried over to Slasher. "You okay?"

Slasher nodded and picked up his helm. "I am now. That venom was nasty. I thought my face was going to burn off. I really think we've outdone ourselves with this game. Almost too real."

"I think that was the point of it," Greensleeves said.

"The realer the better," Steelmaiden handed Slasher back his spear. "That makes it more fun, right?"

Slasher nodded as he put the spear across his back. "At least, we heal quickly in game."

"There is that," Baladara agreed. "'Cause, man these things were nasty."

"And they aren't even the bosses of this level," Steelmaiden added.

Horc squatted down to loot the first one they killed before it vanished. There was a fair amount of meat on it, along with a piece of leather armor. There was also a set of fangs. His display lit up.

1 of 6 Cobra fangs.

He sighed. "Guys, you better all loot these things, they've got fangs we need. We're going to have to kill at least four more."

Slasher rolled his eyes. "Wow, these were what kept killing my party, and we need at least four more. Not cool."

"But they were good for XP," Steelmaiden said.

Horc hadn't been paying attention when the cobras died to see how much XP they got. After the first few things, the XP was almost secondary to the action of killing. He also wasn't totally paying attention to the damage amounts that flashed on his screen. It was something he just wasn't sure really mattered as long as the monsters went down.

As he moved to the second cobra to get his fangs, since Steelmaiden had already pulled the rest of the loot, he wondered if it would help his game playing if he paid more attention to things like damage, both given and taken. He'd be able to better judge his attacks, and he might be able to notice if certain attacks were more effective against certain opponents than others. When they were done looting, he held up the leather vest he'd gotten. "Anyone want this?" Horc looked at the armor. It was a:

Snakeskin Vest,
Leather armor 20
Resist Venom +3
Level 11

The two warriors shook their head. Greensleeves waved it aside.

Baladara sighed. "Sorry, cloth only for me. You keep it. It should be better than what you're wearing."

Horc pulled up his character sheet. His current chest armor was.

Wolf Tunic
Leather armor 10
Level 3

Closing the character sheet, Horc took off his pack and quiver, pulled off his tunic and shoved it into the pack, then slipped on the vest. It was lighter and felt like he could move better.

He looked at his friends. "Well, how do I look?"

Greensleeves chuckled. "Like you're ready for a night at the leather bar."

Horc laughed. "Okay then. Let's keep going, we've got more cobras to kill." As they headed on down the passage way, he wondered if there was any way he'd be able to pick an outfit that he liked and stick with it. He'd been okay with the tunic, but understood how better armor would help him take more damage and stay alive longer. The thing was, he was more of a tunic guy IRL, and not so much the vest sort. Then Baladara crossed his line of sight and he was reminded that IRL Mike was a guy, not a female, and a human, not an elf. The game was all about fantasy. Maybe in his games, he could stop being so focused on making things like real life and just find a way to be the character he created. Was that why he liked science fiction games better—they were something he could aspire to be where fantasy games weren't? He wasn't sure.

AFTER FIGHTING their way through the cobra's special attacks, they were prepared for them and made quick work of the next four they encountered. When another cobra dropped a second vest, Greensleeves took it without complaint. Their coins kept mounting up too. After the last cobra, Horc pulled up his coin purse and looked at it. 10 gold, 5 silver and 65 copper. He wasn't sure what was considered good at level eleven, but he wasn't going to complain.

"I wonder how much farther this level goes," Slasher said as they started off after completing the quest for the fangs.

"So, you didn't make it this far?" Baladara asked.

Slasher shook his head. "We never made it past the first set of cobras. This has all been new to me since then."

"Then there's no reason for you to be at point anymore," Steelmaiden said. "Let's do this together."

"Okay." Slasher acquiesced to her and they stalked down the passageway side by side, a formidable front to their party.

Baladara leaned close to Horc as they walked. "You know, Steelmaiden's really dominant. I bet she and Lisa would get along great."

Horc chuckled. He hadn't met Lisa, but presumed she was good at keeping Mike in line. He figured she and Steelmaiden would either get along great or constantly butt heads.

"Hold up." Steelmaiden held up here hand for them to stop as they came to a turn in the tunnel. "If this thing isn't our level boss, I'm not sure I want to see them."

"What is it?" Greensleeves asked, edging closer so he could peer around the corner. He peered back with pursed lips. "Yeah. That's going to be nasty."

"Steel, do you have a Battle Charge attack?" Slasher asked.

Steelmaiden nodded. "Yeah. Maybe if we both use that to close in fast and furious we can knock her down quickly. Do you want the right and I'll take the left?"

Slasher nodded. "Sure. Sounds like a plan. The rest of you guys get ready to hit her as hard as possible. This may get messy."

Horc eased up and peered around the corner, getting himself locked onto their opponent. **Pricilla Simone Hydra Queen, Level 19** with two stars. That nearly made sense seeing how the snake warrior woman had two heads. Actually, she had two torsos, each with two arms. One set of arms held a bow with a nocked arrow, the other set held a pair of long swords. She looked more than dangerous—she looked downright apocalyptic. Horc's stomach clenched up and he forced himself to breathe. It was going to take a lot of damage to bring her down. She was definitely a major boss, and made it totally understandable why players, even players in parties, were having trouble getting through the dungeon. She also looked like two of the floor supervisors he'd met from the Houston office. Horc didn't take the time to point it out.

"Charge!" Steelmaiden and Slasher shouted at the same time. They took off running around the corner at full speed. Horc readied his own bow and stepped around to watch them slam into the hydra, driving their spears deep into each torso.

The monster rocked back and screamed. Then its hair came alive, just like the Gorgon Priestesses they'd battled earlier.

Horc fired at the snake heads lashing at his party mates.

"Crap, crap, and crap," Baladara said as she cast her first fireball.

Horc's wolf bounded across the distance between them and the hydra. It went toward the torso Steelmaiden was battling as her spectral wolf appeared and joined the fight.

Greensleeves hit the point where the torsos joined together with a ball of green Druid power. The hydra's health had started to drop but not by much.

Horc hoped his Flame Arrow would catch the monster's hair on fire and kept firing, taking out the snake heads as fast as he could. Then the first of the hydra's own arrows hit Horc. Pain seared through him as the arrow sliced his side from front to back. Twenty percent of his health dropped in that one hit.

Horc aimed for her hand holding the bow. He aimed his shot as best he could and caught one of her fingers.

He felt like his life was draining out of him as he fired another shot at her hand, just as she unleashed another arrow at him. Somehow, Horc managed to twist out of the way and got off a third shot, thankful his bow was faster than hers. Her hand spasmed and she dropped the bow as she started yanking arrows out with the hand she'd been loading arrows with.

Horc got off more arrows but felt weaker by the second. His health was disappearing and he wasn't actively taking damage. "What's going on?"

"Ah, man, you've been poisoned," Greensleeves said. "Let me fix that. That's some nasty stuff to hit you that hard with your new vest's buffs."

Horc forced himself to keep firing. If Greensleeves could heal him, he'd be fine. The hydra was doing some major damage to Steelmaiden and Slasher, and although Horc had managed to get about half of the hair on his target to stop moving, it did damage to her, but hadn't dropped her to a quarter health yet.

Slasher shouted and plunged his spear deep into the hydra. Both heads screamed as its health dropped to below a quarter. As long as Greensleeves's mana held out, they had hope of making it through the fight. Slasher jerked his spear up and down, eliciting more screams as the hydra beat at him with her swords. The heavy blows rang out in the marble-tiled passageway but didn't seem to do much in the way of damage to Slasher. His plate armor was doing a great job of protecting him.

Horc kept firing his arrows, doing as much damage as he could to the writhing hair. Pretty soon he had it all dead. The hydra's health was down to a half.

After ramming her spear as hard into the torso that had held the bow as she could, Steelmaiden punched it in the face, and grabbed one of the other torso's swords and ripped it out of her grasp, only to drive it home next to the spear the first torso was trying to pull out.

The torso that had used the bow moved its hands in an attempt to cast a spell.

"Casting!" Baladara shouted as her next Fireball hit the torso.

Without a word, Steelmaiden grabbed her hands and yanked hard. The crack of breaking bones rang out in the passageway. The monster's health dropped below a quarter and began to flash.

"I hate doing this." Baladara pulled her short sword and dashed forward.

Only then did Horc glance at the party icons in the corner of his vision. Steelmaiden's spectral wolf had vanished, it's minute of combat finished. Baladara was out of mana, Greensleeves was fairly close, and his own was desperately under a half. If they didn't finish the hydra off soon, the two fighters were going to be the only ones who could use special attacks. They'd be down to base weapons and that would be hard against the formidable foe.

Greensleeves shouted something, then his body changed. Horc tried to watch, while continuing his attack, but it was hard. One second Greensleeves was standing there, then after Horc finished his Multishot, there was a huge tree-like creature standing in his place. Greensleeves avatar in the group list had changed to resemble the tree thing he'd become, but his mana was higher.

Hoping he'd set the hydra on fire, Horc shot the torso that still had moving hair with a Flame Arrow then followed up with his Multishot. Three heads stopped wiggling and striking. The hydra's health continued flashing an encouraging orange.

Horc's wolf was at Steelmaiden's side, biting and tearing at the monster. Horc kept at work taking out the hair heads. With each one, the hydra weakened more. As much damage as Steelmaiden and Slasher did to its torsos, it appeared that somehow the hair snakes were the key to taking the monster all the way down to nothing.

"Give it a haircut!" Horc sent another volley of arrows at the heads. "The heads do more damage than anything else."

Slasher yanked his spear out of her gut and seconds later it glowed a bright yellow. He shouted something unintelligible and swung up with the spear, neatly slicing off half of the remaining heads.

The hydra queen's health started flashing red. She struggled to throw Steelmaiden, Slasher and the wolf off, but they all stayed tight, fighting her with everything they had. Baladara drove her sword into the spot where the two torsos met, just as the archer side spat at her. The second the spit hit her robes they began to smoke, then Baladara screamed.

"I've got you." Greensleeves limbs were a blue blur as he worked the healing spell. "Get the robe off."

Horc wanted to go help Baladara but knew he couldn't until the hydra was dead. Two more snakeheads still moved on the other torso. He carefully targeted one and let an arrow fly. The hit was good and the snake stopped moving. He reached back for another arrow. His quiver was empty.

"I'm out of arrows!" He pulled his axe and rushed forward. "Only one head left."

"I see it." Steelmaiden sliced the last head off easily.

The hydra queen screamed a death cry, shook violently and crashed to the ground.

They all glowed with the golden glow of leveling.

"Wow! That was incredible." Slasher said. "How did we all manage to level at once?"

"She was worth that many points," Steelmaiden said. "I got over five hundred points for her."

"Over seven hundred for me," Baladara said, "but I'm lower level than you guys. It also really helps that we're several levels below most of these monsters. Even with the party split of points, we're cranking like crazy in here."

"This could only happen in a beta like this where we've all started out within a short time of each other." Shedding his tree form, Greensleeves knelt and started looting the body.

Coins clinked into Horc's pouch. He barely heard it as he pulled his quiver from over his shoulder and stared at the empty leather holder. He was out of ammo. He wasn't sure what he was going to do. It wasn't like he could stop in the middle of a dungeon and run to a vendor to get more. He'd gotten as many as he could carry before they'd headed out from town and it wasn't enough.

"Horc, catch." Greensleeves tossed him something.

Reflexively, Horc grabbed the wrapped leather out of the air. He paused, it was the quiver from the bow wielding torso. It was full of arrows. He beamed. Then he looked at it closer.

Everfull Quiver:

Quiver will always have at least one arrow of each type you put in it.

Poison Arrow — +3 poison damage per second for ten seconds

Impact Arrow — Renders target stunned for three seconds

Razor Arrow — 10 damage + 5% chance of bleed out for 5 seconds for additional 3 damage per second.

Horc couldn't believe his eyes. There were regular arrows in one slot and still two empty slots for other arrows. "Are you guys sure?"

Greensleeves stood and held up a silver circlet. "You're our only archer and you've run out of arrows, of course I'm sure. I don't think anyone else is going to complain. Now, before she disappears, loot for the Hydra Queen's circlet, You'll find it's a quest item."

Horc bent over the body and retrieved the circlet and the quest completed on his screen. With a heavy sigh, Horc sank down onto the marble floor, pulling out a water-skin and took a long drink. His mana slowly rose. Around him, the others were doing the same, although Slasher and Steelmaiden were also eating. It took them a few minutes before everyone was back to good condition.

"Well, I hope that was our big boss for this level," Greensleeves said as he closed his pack and slipped it back on his back.

"If not, we'll kick the boss's butt and go on," Slasher said. "You guys are really good at this."

"We're doing our best with what we've got," Steelmaiden said. She held up the two swords she'd gotten from the hydra. "Do you mind if I keep these? I don't know if you can dual wield or not, but I can, and together they are just a little better than the spear. That way we've got one of us doing piercing damage and one doing cutting damage."

Slasher nodded thoughtfully. "That might come in handy. Sure, keep them."

"Thanks." She grinned as she put the spear in her pack and crossed the swords across her back. "So what do you guys say to us finding the next door and keeping going while the going is good?"

Baladara was trying to mend her burned and torn robe. "Just a minute. This thing's a mess."

"Hey, hold on. It wasn't a major find, so I didn't say anything, but I think I picked up another robe back a few priestesses ago." Steelmaiden dug into her pack, then pulled out a purple robe. "Will this help?"

Baladara grinned. "Yeah, it will." She wadded the old robe up and crammed it into her pack. "Not much of an improvement, but anything will do right now." She yanked the new robe over her head, then slung her pack on her back. "Now, I'm ready to go."

Horc glanced at Greensleeves. "Hey was that tree thing you pulled your special shapechanging healer power?"

Greensleeves nodded. "Cool huh. It doesn't take much in the way of mana to cast, and doubles the mana at the time of casting. It also drops the cost of mana for healing and restoration spells. The drawback is it drops the damage I can do with my attack spells. So since our party needs every attack we can get, I've been reserving it until I have to use it."

"Good call." Steelmaiden grinned as she pointed her sword in the direction they were heading. "Now, let's get moving."

They started off down the passage again, and soon came to another door. Hopefully it indicated the end of level two and the start of level three.

"Hey, I might have the key for that," Slasher said. "I got it in a drop before my original party deserted me." He reached in his pack and pulled out a purple crystal shaped like a pyramid. "I'm guessing you guys found a blue egg on the first level."

Horc nodded. "Yeah, and it opened the door easily."

Like the first door, the new one had an indentation in it, but it was square going toward a point at the center.

"Okay. Let's see if this works like the other one did." Slasher put the crystal into the hole. There was a soft click, and then a deep purple light danced over the door that slid open slightly.

"I guess we've got that figured out," Greensleeves said, leaning on his staff. "As long as we get the right drops, it's working out pretty easily, although after the first level, I figured it would be a boss drop."

Slasher pulled the crystal out of the door and put it in his pack. "Nope. I got this off of some of those bitches close to the start of the level."

"Then it might not be that easy," Baladara said. "We might want to make sure we kill everything we can find until we get the crystal drop, if each level is going to require that to keep going down. Man, I wish the wiki was complete and could've warned us about this development."

"Then we just update the wiki when we get out of here," Greensleeves said. "Let's keep moving."

Horc wished they had more information too. If they'd known what all they were going to run into, he might've waited another couple or five levels before coming in. Grinding on the wolves, pigs and bears might've been boring, but he would've been better prepared.

20

BEYOND THE door, the marble floor they'd been on since they left the stairs fell away and a rough dirt floor led them on deeper down into the mountain they had entered many stories above. Everything seemed to weigh in on Horc. The air grew mustier as they continued their journey. The new passageway curved back in on itself, making it nearly impossible to see more than a few feet at a time. Horc was lucky to be in the middle of the group, but he was fairly sure that Steelmaiden couldn't see Greensleeves if she stopped and looked over her shoulder. The passageway also grew steeper as they went, as if it were trying to hurry them along to whatever waited for them at the bottom.

Steelmaiden stopped at the bottom. "Wait a minute."

The rest of the party clustered behind her.

"What's up?" Horc asked.

"We've got movement not far from here." Steelmaiden pulled her swords. "Everyone be ready."

Horc nocked an arrow and readied to shoot. Greensleeves's hands glowed with a spell ready to cast, as did Baladara's. Slasher's hands tightened on his spear.

"Let's go." Steelmaiden jumped around the corner.

Horc and the others followed, his wolf staying close at his heels.

The cavern was full of mushrooms. They varied in size and color. Some were massive red with white undersides and white spots. Others were small gray and smooth. There were huge green ones, and tiny blue ones. They covered the ground and grew out of the walls. A few of the pointed gray ones even grew upside down from the ceiling.

"Wow, where did they come up with the idea for this place?" Horc asked as his gaze traveled the cavern.

"They spent a lot of time coming up a lot of new ideas, but also drawing from classic science fiction and fantasy works," Greensleeves said.

Something screamed and rushed toward them. Horc targeted it. The text flashed **Bugbear Warrior, level 16**. It was huge, more bear than warrior. Its face was long and distorted, almost canine with extreme fangs from both sides of its slathering jaws. It carried a short spear that looked as battered as its torn, piecemeal leather armor. Long brown hair covered every visible part of its hide and poked out from the gaps in its armor.

Steelmaiden slashed it and the rest of them unleashed their own attacks. Balls of Druid and Mage energy hit it at the same time Horc's Multishot barrage struck. The bugbear's health dropped to half almost instantly, then Slasher and the wolf connected with it and pushed it back. Two more rounds of attacks and it dropped dead.

"That was nearly too easy," Slasher said as Steelmaiden looted the corpse.

"Maybe we got lucky?" Horc said.

"We might've all dealt critical damage at the same time," Greensleeves said as he cast his healing on Steelmaiden.

"I'd be surprised at that," Baladara said.

"Let's see what happens with the next couple," Steelmaiden said as she wiped down her blades. "Unfortunately, not only was it easy to kill, it didn't have much in the way of loot."

"Then we kill more of them," Slasher said.

Greensleeves bent and picked up a few mushrooms and slipped them into his pack. "At least there's lots of herbs in this area, things I've never seen before."

"We have to be careful," Steelmaiden said and stepped away as the bugbear's corpse vanished in a cloud of pixels.

They fell into a tight formation behind her, with Slasher bringing up the rear.

Horc kept his bow in hand with an arrow ready to fly. His nerves were strung tight as they stalked through the strange fungal forest. His mind kept playing tricks on him; he thought that the shadows were moving and gazes were following him. The sounds of the mushroom forest were muffled; even Slasher's heavy footsteps were muted by the thick peat they crossed.

Multiple shouts surrounded them and a mass of bugbears swarmed them.

Horc was only able to fire one arrow before they were too close. He dropped his bow and pulled his axe as the wolf brought one down. Horc swung his axe hard and fast. Bugbear blood sprayed out from the wound. Then the wolf pulled him down.

Steelmaiden shouted, and as her spectral wolf appeared, three of the bugbears converged on her, but many more were still around, attacking the rest of the party. As Horc's first one fell, he looked for the next closest one.

Baladara hit one with a Fireball. It stumbled back and bumped Horc who spun and buried his axe in the monster's arm, cleaving both leather and skin easily. He wished the beast would back up so he could use an arrow or four. The bugbear swung a rusty sword. It caught Horc in the shoulder. The blow ached, but the sword didn't have enough of an edge to get through his leather armor. Horc hit it again with his axe. His wolf savaged it. The bugbear howled, for a moment, sounding more like a wolf than a monster. Horc hit it again, trying to aim his blow to strike the creature's hairy, bullish neck where there wasn't any armor. It hit him again. Its health was less than half gone, but his own was down by a quarter. He hit the beast in the arm, trying to dislodge its weapon. The bugbear bit him, sinking its massive fangs into his shoulder. Horc screamed. His wolf leapt on the bugbear. It off-balanced them both. The three of them crashed to the ground with Horc and the wolf on top. The change of angle forced the beast's fangs out of Horc's shoulder. The bugbear's health bar began to flash orange. His health was nearly at half. Horc hit it again with his axe. The blade sank into the monster's face, caving in its nose. Its health went red. The bugbear continued to struggle even as it got closer to death. It hit Horc in the side of the head. The blow stunned him for a moment. His wolf's jaws clamped down on the monster's neck and ended its life.

Horc jerked back and reached into his pack to pull out a healing potion. He didn't want to distract Greensleeves from his own fight. The potion tasted like sweet cherry juice. It bumped up his health to nearly one hundred percent.

He stood and swung his axe at the closest monster, one attacking Baladara. Its health was already at half. The axe bit into its neck at the base of its head. The bugbear screamed and reached back as if to hit Horc. Then it jerked hard. Baladara jabbed her sword deep in its chest. Its health flashed orange. Horc hit it again in the head. Its blood sprayed out. Its health dropped to nothing and it fell over.

Pulling out another potion from his bag, Horc handed it to Baladara. "You did pretty good with these."

Baladara took the potion and downed it. "Thanks. Let's keep killing these fools."

"Don't worry," Steelmaiden said. "We got the rest of them." She sounded tired.

"Then let's get these things looted and restore everyone's health and mana." Greensleeves appeared behind Steelmaiden. "But I think we should keep an eye or two open while we do that. There's probably more of them out there."

"You got that right," Steelmaiden said. "So, you drink first. We need our healer ready to roll."

While they ate and drank, Horc looted the corpses. As Steelmaiden had noticed on the first one, there wasn't much on them. A few coins, some food and drinks, and bad weapons. He debated leaving the weapons, but still had the bag space to spare, so he kept them in case he could get anything for them from vendors. The last one he looted vanished within seconds. If he'd been a little slower, he'd have missed the loot.

"Let's keep moving," Steelmaiden said. "Too much of a chance for another ambush if we sit here too long. We need to find key and the boss for this level so we can get done here."

HORC LOST track of how many ambushes they walked into. The close-quarter fighting made it hard for him to get off any arrows. He was getting good with his axe, but wished he had some kind of magic he could work on his hand to hand to make it more effective like his arrows. Even understanding he wasn't a tank like Steelmaiden and Slasher, he would've liked to do more when he was forced to engage in close quarters. Those times he thought his wolf did more damage than he did, but didn't really pay close attention to their health bars when he was fighting the bugbears, since he was in the middle of battle, and that took up most of his attention.

"Okay, folks, the mushrooms are thinning out," Steelmaiden said as they approached one really thick red stalk. "Hopefully we can avoid any more major ambushes."

"That would be nice," Baladara said. "They're getting old." She rubbed her hand across the torn sleeve of her new robe. "I'm not great at hand-to-hand combat. That's why I'm a mage."

They made it around the stalk and found themselves on the bank of an underground river. There was thick green moss along the bank and the river was a good ten feet across with another moss-covered bank on the other side, before the mushroom forest started up again.

Steelmaiden frowned at the river. "It's too wide to jump and I'm not sure how deep it is."

"We won't know until we try," Slasher said and jumped in. He promptly sank from view.

"Slasher!" Greensleeves dove in after him. He disappeared for a moment, then resurfaced. "He's walking along the bottom of the river." He then turned and swam to the other side.

Steelmaiden huffed. "Yeah, you can't swim in plate armor. I don't know if I can swim in this light mail. I guess we'll see." She jumped in. She bobbed for a second, then sank down as she started swimming.

"Look out, there's crocodiles in the river," Greensleeves shouted as he climbed out on the other side. He turned back to the river and cast a ball of green Druid magic.

"Where?" Horc peered into the river. He couldn't see very far into the water. As far as he could tell, there wasn't anything in there.

Steelmaiden popped up about halfway across the river. "Could use a hand here."

"I can't target what I can't see," Horc shouted back. He kept scanning the waters around her.

"There is it!" Baladara yelled as her hands glowed red with her casting.

A reptilian head surfaced next to Steelmaiden. **River Crocodile, Level 15**. Horc shot an Impact Arrow at it. The croc stopped moving for a second, then Baladara's

Fireball hit it. Steelmaiden struggled to stay above the water as she tried to get a solid blow against the beast.

"Where's Slasher?" Horc hollered across the river as he hit the croc with a Razor Arrow and a Flame spell. The thing burst into flames that didn't seem to be deterred by the water. The croc's health had dropped to between a quarter and a half.

"Down on the bottom fighting another one," Steelmaiden said. "We need to finish this one off so I can aggro the other one." She stabbed a sword through the croc's head. Its health flashed orange.

Horc's wolf was swimming out toward her. Horc fired a Multishot at the same time Greensleeves hit it with another ball of Druid magic. The croc died and floated along the surface of the water.

"I've got you targeted for healing," Greensleeves shouted. "Go get Slasher."

Steelmaiden gave him a quick wave and dove down.

"This isn't good," Horc said. "How long can he hold his breath?"

Baladara shrugged. "It's a game, so it's not really how long he can hold his breath, but how much time the game gives him before he runs out of air…it's slightly different. Okay. Here she comes." She pointed at the river as Steelmaiden resurfaced. "I managed to aggro it."

The crocodile surfaced and Horc could get a lock on it. He started with an Impact Arrow, then a Flaming Razor Arrow. The croc had been about down when it surfaced. It only took one round of attacks from the full party for it to die.

As it went belly up, something surged out of the water on the far bank.

"Slasher!" Greensleeves rushed over, his hands casting a blue healing spell as he ran.

Horc glanced at the party display, Slasher's health was flashing red and had only the faintest of slivers left. Then his health bar steadily rose.

"What do you think we should do?" Horc asked as he and Baladara waited on the bank of the river as his wolf swam back over to him.

"Move fast," Baladara said. "If we're lucky there were just two of them and we can get across before they respawn, but then this is a dungeon, things aren't respawning quickly, but just to be safe." She dove in the water.

Horc frowned at the river. He wasn't a great swimmer IRL. It had been years since he'd even been in a swimming pool. He didn't like swimming in rivers and lakes. But Halfworld was a game, not real life. He squared his shoulders and hoped that Half Orcs could swim. He jumped in.

The river water was cold, and Horc dog-paddled next to his wolf across the river. He was nearly there when two large lumbering monsters that looked like they were part of a bog rushed out of the mushroom forest toward the party standing on the shore watching him.

"Behind you!" Horc raised a hand and tried to point, but he lost his forward momentum and sank slightly. Water went in his mouth and he blew out a stream as he resurfaced.

On the bank he was headed toward, his party had turned and were engaging the two creatures. With more determination, Horc focused on getting himself across the river so he could get out of the water and help them. His wolf made it out first, and stood on the bank waiting for him.

As soon as he cleared the water, Horc drew his bow, hoping it would work right with a wet string. He reminded himself it was a game and not reality, no matter how much things like the cold of the water seeped into him and he could smell the rotting stench of the bog monsters a few feet away.

Targeting the first one showed **Putrid Bog Beast, level 18**. His bow string was tight as ever and he launched an Impact Arrow, slowing one of the creatures. He hit the other with another Impact Arrow and grinned as Steelmaiden laid into it with both swords slashing. His wolf ran between the two attacking almost as fast as Horc's arrows.

"We're in a mushroom swamp," Baladara said as she slung Fireballs at the bog beasts. "I guess rotting heaps of vegetation that attack us shouldn't be a big surprise."

"Probably not." Horc's Razor Arrow, Flame Arrow combo knocked one down to half and set it on fire. The fire seemed to burn hotter than normal and the damage it did dropped the thing to a quarter the next round.

Baladara hit it with another Fireball and the thing collapsed under Slasher's spear.

Without waiting for anyone to say anything, Horc switched to the second monster. His Flame Arrow did a decent amount of damage, but didn't set it on fire. He had to keep firing as the others swarmed it, quickly rendering it into a huge pile of sliced and scorched greens.

They quickly set to looting them. Greensleeves cheered. "Hey, it's almost like skinning for Horc. These things give herbs. Extra bonus!"

"But are they things I can use?" Baladara asked. "I looked during our last rest and I can't find recipes I can use the mushrooms in. I know they say they're good for potions, but what potions?"

Greensleeves kept pulling bits of strange vegetation off the corpses until they started to vanish. "I've got no idea, but we've got the goods for once you figure out what you can use them on, or maybe I'll find a Witch to sell them to or put them up in the flea market. They have to be good for something." He shoved the two handfuls of plant matter into his pack.

"We can sort everything out once we beat this dungeon and get back to the city," Steelmaiden said.

Horc nodded, liking the idea of keeping moving. "So which way?"

Steelmaiden frowned. "Not exactly sure. I've been trying to keep us going in a straight line since we got to the forest, but it's so tight in here I'm having trouble with directions."

"How about you?" Slasher asked. "You're a Ranger. Do you have any kind of direction sense or anything?"

Horc frowned. "Should I?"

"I don't know about Halfworld, but in some games, Rangers and Druids both have a sense of direction," Greensleeves said. "I don't seem to have it, and I don't remember seeing it on your character sheet back at the Inn. If we keep an eye on the map, it should help."

"But we don't know where the door is," Steelmaiden replied. "I mean we can see where we've been, but not where we're going."

"Good point." Horc looked around. So many of the mushrooms looked alike to him. If it wasn't for the trail they were leaving through trampled moss, he wouldn't have known where they'd been. The previous levels had been mostly passageways had been easier to navigate, or at least get to where they wanted to go. They had to find the door, and the crystal that opened it.

As if reading his thoughts about finding the crystal as well as the door, Greensleeves said. "Let's just keep going through the mobs we find and see about getting the crystal. Once we have it, we can worry about finding the door."

Steelmaiden grinned. "Sounds like a plan to me." She stomped off into the mushrooms.

Horc and the others followed her, weapons ready for anything that might come at them. The dungeon seemed to go on forever, and Horc was thankful for the sleep he'd gotten the night before, even with the pod keeping his body alive, he didn't want to think about how tired he'd have been if he'd really been in the dungeon they were fighting their way through.

21

"HEY, THIS looks like a wall," Steelmaiden called out as they reached a spot where the forest ended.

"But still no key or door," Horc said as he approached the stone cave wall. It looked a lot like the walls of the passageways they'd seen other places in the dungeon, but had mushrooms growing around the rocks and boulders in scattered patches.

"Why don't we just follow the wall around and find the door?" Greensleeves suggested. "Once we can mark it on the map, we can look around for the boss and hopefully find the key while we're going around."

Slasher pursed his lips and nodded. "I like the sound of that. Making progress is better than just wandering around aimlessly hoping we find something."

"Then let's keep moving," Steelmaiden said and started off along the wall. There was a narrow pathway that was clear of mushrooms that were big enough to block their passage. Of all the other areas of Halfworld they'd been in up until that point, it showed the first signs of being designed and not just random nature.

The wall continued on. The walking was faster in the cleared area than it was in the close-growing mushrooms. Before they found the door, they encountered three more ambushes. They kept coming. The bugbears seemed fearless and unyielding in their attacks on the party. They made Horc wonder what they would've been like in the real world, had there ever been creatures like what they battled outside of a game. The game was so real, it made him think how could people come up with all the small details like the underveins of the mushrooms and the tiny tendrils of the moss? In some ways, the early games had it easier. They didn't have to worry as much about the minutiae as the developers of the VR games did. The VR developers obviously spent lots of time studying the real world to get everything right in the game world so players didn't spot the flaws.

"Over here," Steelmaiden called. "Looks like we found the door."

They gathered around the door; there was a small square indentation in the middle of the door, just like the keyholes in the other doors.

"Looks like we need to find a cube of some kind," Baladara said. "I'm guessing nobody has found a crystal cube in their looting."

"I haven't," Slasher said.

"Not me," Greensleeves added.

"Nothing for me," Steelmaiden said.

Horc shook his head. "We also haven't found the boss yet."

"Then let see about doing both." Steelmaiden turned from the door.

"If we're going to get through this dungeon, we're going to have to." Greensleeves gripped his staff and followed her.

There was a tension there that made Horc wonder if Greensleeves wasn't getting tired too. It would've been nice if things would go smoother, but if it was too smooth, it wouldn't be as interesting for a lot of players. Horc wasn't exactly ready to tell the others that he was having more fun in the game than he expected to. In the dungeon, fighting for his life, it was easy for him to forget what was happening to him outside the game.

"ACCORDING TO the map, there's not much more of this area that we haven't explored," Greensleeves said as they paused near the river they had crossed three times. "Let's hit this spot and see what's going on there." Greensleeves tapped a spot on the map and a dot appeared on Horc's map. The place wasn't far from where they were.

"Then let's find the boss we're looking for," Steelmaiden said. "I just hope he has the key, it's been a little while since we've encountered any mobs. I think we're getting close to cleaning out this place."

"I was thinking that too." Baladara grinned. "The more monsters we off, the fewer options we're going to have to find the key."

"Then let's hope it drops quickly." Greensleeves headed away from the river, toward the unexplored area.

After moving through the mushroom forest for several more minutes, a small village came into view. The huts were fairly basic grass huts with thatched roofs. There were bugbears around, moving in and out of the huts. Most of them were levels fifteen to eighteen. One, larger and grayer than the others looked like the one they needed. **Chief Samsallan, level 20**. There were two stars next to his name. His face was a dead likeness for the IT manager from the Dallas office. Horc was pretty sure Sam Sallan would find out. He was a fairly active gamer, but he had a good sense of humor and would probably think it was great having a dungeon boss named after and looking like him.

"We're going to need to pull these guys one or two at a time, if we have to," Slasher said. "Ranger Horc, you're our best option for that."

Horc nodded. He understood what was needed. They'd done the maneuver a few times in the forest outside the dungeon when they were hunting the Gnolls there. Pulling a Razor Arrow, he scanned the village for the closest bugbear he could target. One bugbear, a level sixteen, walked out of a hut at the edge of the village.

There were no other monsters close. Horc fired his arrow. It cut deep into the bugbear, dropping its health a good chunk. The beast turned and ran toward Horc and the party. Horc's wolf raced to meet it. The wolf, Horc's second arrow, Greensleeve's Druid magic bolt, Baladara's Fireball, all hit at nearly the same time. They knocked the beast down to the orange zone instantly. It continued to charge and Horc's next round with a Flame Arrow took it out.

Slasher rushed out and looted it.

A soft clink of coins sounded as Horc looked for his next target. For several minutes, it went as they planned-- pulling a bugbear or two at a time and killing them easily. With the number of occupants in the village and the others from the forest, they'd killed more mobs in that level of the dungeon than in all the others combined.

Baladara was the first to level, going up to level eleven. Then Horc rolled up to level thirteen. Two kills later, Greensleeves hit fourteen. The next kill leveled Steelmaiden to fourteen, then when they pulled three at one time, Slasher hit fourteen as well.

The chief hadn't gotten close enough to pull. It was like he knew where Horc was and was determined to stay just out of his range.

"We're going to need to get closer," Slasher said, after looting the most recent kill. "Let's use the huts for cover."

Steelmaiden nodded. "Sounds good."

With more nods, they followed Slasher toward the nearest hut. They reached it without incident. Slasher waved them to cut around both sides of the hut. They got to the side and glanced out into the middle of the village. The only visible bugbears were the ones across the village. They needed to get closer for him to pull more. When Slasher glanced around the hut from the other side, Horc gestured with his bow for them to move closer.

Slasher gave him a thumbs up and turned back. Seconds later, Slasher, and Greensleeves darted across the opening between the huts to the next one, moving closer to the center of the village.

Once they were there, Steelmaiden led Horc and Baladara across to the same hut. They again circled the hut. There wasn't anything but open ground between them and the village center. Horc spotted Chief Samsallan and managed to get a target lock on him. He had a Razor Arrow already nocked and added flames to it. He fired quickly, before the chief could get out of range. The arrow hit hard and fast. His wolf followed it across the open space as Greensleeves and Baladara cast their spells. Slasher and Steelmaiden moved to intercept the bugbear as he charged their hiding place. Their swords and spear connected with the bugbear chief as Horc got a Multishot of Impact Arrows into him. The chief's health began to drop, but it was slow. They all continued to attack him, then suddenly, when they'd managed to drop him below half, his health began to rise.

"What's happening?" Horc asked as he fired another Impact Arrow to keep the chief moving slowly.

"There must be a priest, or shaman, or someone who's healing him faster than we can damage him." Greensleeves said.

"Then let's find him," Slasher jabbed the chief again, and ran toward Baladara. "Greensleeves, keep Steelmaiden alive and fighting. We'll find this healer and take him out."

A knot formed in Horc's gut at the idea of the two of them going off by themselves, but it was the best option, otherwise the caster would be able to keep healing the chief and the battle would come down to who ran out of mana first.

His next Flame Arrow caught the chief on fire. The big bug bear howled in pain. A shout went up from a nearby hut. A smaller bugbear charged out and went after Steelmaiden. Seconds later her spectral wolf appeared and joined the fight, going for the one heading in Steelmaiden's direction.

Horc changed targets quickly and hit it with an Impact Arrow. The level sixteen slowed as Horc's wolf left his assault of the chief and hit it, followed by Greensleeves' attack.

For several minutes, Horc alternated between the smaller bugbear and the chief, hitting them with arrows, Flaming and Razor Arrows first, then Impact Arrows whenever the bugbears started moving. His mana was dropping quickly. But both bugbears' health was dropping fast too. His wolf howled. Its health was nearly gone. Horc shot off an arrow at the chief, then cast his Heal Companion spell. It didn't totally heal the wolf, but did a good job of bringing it to almost seventy five percent. The wolf finished off the smaller bugbear, but Horc was out of mana. He used his Razor Arrows and Impact Arrows as fast as he could, cutting the chief down as far and fast as he could while Steelmaiden continued to slash away at him.

After firing an Impact Arrow, Horc chanced a glance at the team icons. Baladara was out of mana and getting close to dying. Slasher was fairly low too. Horc glanced around and couldn't spot either one of them.

The chief was nearly down and so far hadn't been healed again. Horc took that as a good sign. "Greensleeves, find Baladara and Slasher." His mana restored just enough, Horc fired another Razor Arrow with flames. It cut the chief deep and set him on fire. His health flashed orange, then red as Steelmaiden got in a major blow. Horc fired one last Impact Arrow and the chief's life flashed its last red and he dropped.

"Loot quickly and let's help the others," Horc ran past Steelmaiden and looked around in the open area of the village. Four bugbears were piling on the others. As a clink of coins sounded from his pouch, Horc pulled out a healing potion from his pack. "Here!" He tossed it to Steelmaiden who caught it easily.

"Thanks." She upended the potion, then shoved several things into her pack.

Horc pulled out a few more potions and readied to toss them once he slowed some of the bugbears. Pulling an arrow with three vials in his hand wasn't easy, but luckily they were small test-tube size. He fired two Impact Arrows quickly and two of the bugbears slowed to a crawl. His wolf dashed in and started to work on them.

Matching Slasher blow for blow was another large bugbear, but he wasn't quite as big as the chief had been. Horc targeted him. **Mystic Wamalou, level 19**. There was one star next to his name. Inwardly Horc groaned. They were all nearly out of mana and this guy was another bad ass. His face bore a resemblance to the IT manager from Portland. He hit him with an Impact Arrow. Wamalou gestured, the arrow hit him. But didn't seem to slow him down, although it did knock his health down slightly.

Wishing the potions were mana and not just health, Horc made it to Greensleeves first. "Here, you need this." He bashed the bugbear directly in front of Greensleeves in the face with his bow and made it back up.

"Thanks." Greensleeves grabbed the vial and drank it quickly. His health bounced up to half. He swung his staff hard at the bugbear threatening Baladara. Horc hit it with his bow too, then handed Baladara a potion. Her health was nearly full after she drank the potion. Horc fired another Impact Arrow at the mystic, then one at the bugbear next to him. This time the mystic slowed. Slasher jabbed his spear deep into the bugbear, then lifted him off the ground with the weapon still in his gut.

Horc fired again and the mystic was done for.

The remaining bugbears suddenly turned and ran into the mushroom forest. Horc wanted to chase after them, but his friends were in need of rest and recharging before they'd be ready for another round of battle. He dashed to Slasher and handed him the potion. Once again, Slasher's health was in the red.

"Thanks, Dude." Slasher downed the potion. Then sighed. "Looks like we're out of battle for the moment."

Greensleeves came over and nodded. "Looks that way. Let's loot and eat and drink. We need more mana if the key isn't on one of these bodies." He knelt next to the mystic. There was another clinking in the purses. "Does anyone mind if I keep this?" He held up a huge mace with lots of runes on it. "It's a bit better than my staff."

"I think you've earned it," Steelmaiden said. "We've made it through three levels of this dungeon so far and none of us have died. Plus, you haven't claimed anything major yet."

"Thanks." Greensleeves slipped his staff into his pack, then hung the mace on his belt.

"Here it is!" Baladara shouted from behind them. She was kneeling at the body of one of the smaller bugbears. In her upraised hand was a radiant green cube. "We can get out of this level."

Slasher sighed as he pulled out an apple from his pack and took a bite. "It's about time."

Horc had to agree, but each level had gotten harder and harder. Would they all manage to survive the last two levels of the dungeon?

22

HORC PAUSED just inside the door to the next level. There were no stairs, no curving passageway leading down, it just opened into an empty room. It felt wrong somehow. The hairs on the back of Horc's neck stood up. He wanted to turn and go back to the bugbears' village and head out of the dungeon.

"What's wrong?" Baladara asked, pushed Horc slightly to get him to take another step into the empty space.

The place reminded Horc of an empty warehouse, or an unfinished grand porch.

"Something's off," Greensleeves said stepping up beside him. "This doesn't look like any of the rest of the dungeon."

"The rest of the dungeon didn't look like anything in particular," Slasher said as he started across the floor that sounded like it might be wood plank.

"Each one of these has been different," Steelmaiden said, following Slasher.

"Yeah, but they've all had…" Horc struggled to find the right word. "I don't know, a fantasy feel to them, this doesn't, this feels industrial. Manmade."

Steelmaiden stopped and turned back to him. "Well, maybe this level hasn't been finished yet. Maybe the game designers are still working on it. That might be a good thing for Greensleeves to ask his husband."

Slasher was halfway across the room. "Look, if there's nothing beyond this door over here, then we'll know there's a problem with this level, and Greensleeves can log out for a couple of minutes and ask. No-" his words were cut short as the floor collapsed under him and he fell from view.

Steelmaiden and Baladara jumped back, rushing back to where Horc and Greensleeves were standing still just inside the doorway. Behind them the door slammed shut and the sound of a loud click, like a lock being thrown, rang through the empty space.

"Shit," Horc rushed over to the edge of the new hole in the floor with his wolf at his heels. "Slasher, you down there?"

Sharp spikes filled the bottom of the pit. One of them impaled Slasher in the shoulder. Blood poured out of him and his health bar was rapidly dropping.

"Down here—could use some help," Slasher said.

"I've got the healing," Greensleeves called out as a blue aura grew around his hands and he started casting his healing spell.

"Come on, Horc," Steelmaiden said as she eased to the edge of the pit. "Let's go down there and pull him off that spike. I hate pit traps, they're always what DMs use when they can't think of anything else to slow players down. They suck."

Horc sat on the edge of the pit. It was about twenty or so feet down; he wasn't exactly sure. "What's the best way to get down?" He was used to having either a jet pack or hover boots when he was faced with major falls in a game.

"Let me help with that." Baladara stood next to him. "I think I can get you two down with no damage."

"No damage is good," Steelmaiden said.

"Then you get to go first." Baladara cast a spell. Her hands glowed silver and Steelmaiden rose a couple of inches off the floor, then floated down into the pit.

"That worked great," Steelmaiden called up from in the pit. "Horc next."

"Would you guys just hurry?" Slasher asked, sounding pained. "Having a spike through my shoulder wasn't how I planned on spending the evening and being in a pod is making this all the more painful."

As Horc floated into the pit under the power of Baladara's spell, he wondered exactly how much damage Slasher's body was enduring from the wound. A lot of people said the pods didn't do any lasting damage and if someone stayed in them long enough after a wound was healed in a game, they'd never know they'd been damaged IRL. He hoped that was the case, because he knew from his own play that sometimes he was sore for days after he took a blaster hit, even after he'd been healed and everything was fine in game.

Horc landed and hurried between the spikes to where Slasher hung awkwardly, using his good arm to keep from sliding farther down the spike and doing more damage. Greensleeves was on the rim of the pit, continually casting healing spells, but the damage from the spike was all but drinking in each time he finished one.

"I'll get his side closest to the spike," Steelmaiden said when they were in position to lift Slasher free of the spike.

"Good." Horc nodded. He grabbed Slasher's uninjured shoulder, thankful the spikes were about chest high on him. "Ready, set, go."

The two of them heaved Slasher up. His armor screeched against the wood. It was a horrible racket. The only thing worse would be if the spikes had been stone and not wood.

They got him clear and propped up against a neighboring spike. Another one of Greensleeves' healing spells wrapped him in blue and the blood flow from his armor stopped and his health bar stabilized.

"How are you feeling?" Steelmaiden asked.

"Hurts like hell," Slasher replied, reaching up as if to rub his shoulder, but brushing his fingers along his armor.

"I bet." Horc straightened and glanced around the pit. Through the cluster of spikes, the edges of a door peeked out. "Hey, there's a door down here."

"Where?" Steelmaiden stepped next to him and peered. "Ah, there. Hold on, let me check that out." She marched over.

"Is that a good idea?" Baladara shouted down from the lip of the pit.

"It's a dungeon; maybe this pit trap was more than just a way to be really irritating." Steelmaiden didn't stop until she got to the door. She opened it and after a second, peered in. "I've got some stairs going up and going down."

"Up?" Baladara disappeared from Horc's view. "Give me a second to check something." The sound of her running across the floor reverberated in the pit.

"Did you just open that door up there?" Steelmaiden shouted.

"That was me!" Baladara replied. "Looks like our two doors meet and then go on down."

Steelmaiden leaned on the door frame and sighed. "I really do hate pit traps."

HORC WASN'T overly surprised that the stairs went down a fair distance before reaching the bottom. Long stairs were the norm in the dungeon of the Gnoll king. It would be interesting to find out if other dungeons in Halfworld would be similar, or if they were all going to be different. It would be great if they were all at least a little bit different. That would help keep the game interesting for him and the other players, and interesting games helped companies grow. Keeping Total Immersion Systems growing would benefit him IRL and keeping

Halfworld growing and changing might keep him entertained. Even though he was getting tired and ready to head back to the inn, he was totally enjoying the unexpected challenges of the dungeon.

Steelmaiden stopped a couple of feet from the foot of the stairs. "Well that looks promising." She didn't sound the least bit convincing. "I thought we were supposed to be dealing with Gnolls down here. Sure, a lot of time Bugbears and Gnolls are allies, but this just seems to be getting more and more complex." She pointed at a stone wall that covered the passageway. "What do you guys think? I think it's a labyrinth."

Greensleeves nodded. "Yeah, looks that way to me."

Horc stared at the wall. There was enough space for two people to walk side by side between the stone wall and the cave wall. The stone barrier was high enough to reach the ceiling. It looked like they had choices on which way to go.

"I'm not sure if I like this better than the mushroom forest or not," Baladara snipped. "At least the mushrooms were different and interesting. If this wall is like other labyrinths I've been in, the walls are all going to look the same until we reach the center, or end."

"Other than right or left, it doesn't look like we have much choice here," Slayer said. "Which way?"

Horc's wolf walked a couple of paces down the wall to the right, and looked back over its shoulder.

"Let's go right," Horc said, and took out after the wolf.

Baladara followed him. "If the wiki for this game was complete and running right, we could pull that up and use it, but either there hasn't been a lot of time for people to get files updated, or the players who've finished this dungeon haven't taken time to make any notes about it."

"Probably a bit of both," Horc said. He didn't have any experience with beta testing games, but he figured a lot of players who did that enjoyed not having the option to have everything mapped out for them in the dungeons and other parts of the game.

"You know, I think I'm going to do the wiki for this dungeon," Baladara said. "Who knows, Total Immersion Systems might decide to throw in a little extra cash for good wiki posts. That would be helpful."

"It would." Horc paused as they reached the end of the passage way and the wall had an opening to the left.

His wolf stood there with hackles raised, growling.

Horc put a hand on the wolf, stroking its soft fur. "What is it, boy?"

"I bet he knows there's something on the other side of the wall," Steelmaiden said, and walked around them with her sword out.

"Probably." Horc debated for a moment if he should round the corner with his bow out, or his axe. Would the labyrinth be like some of the previous fighting and too tight for slinging arrows at the creatures they encountered?

Steelmaiden glanced at Slayer. "Let's see what this is."

With a nod, Slayer hurried to her side and then they went around the corner. Seconds later, after her War Cry, the sound of steel on steel rang out. It didn't sound like it was right at the turn in the wall.

Drawing his bow string tight, Horc went around the corner. At his side, both Baladara and Greensleeves had their spells started. Steelmaiden and Slasher had already started hacking away at five Gnolls. The text above their heads all read **Gnoll Defender, level 14** with two stars.

Horc cast Flame on his Impact Arrow as he let it fly at the Gnoll Slayer was laying into. It knocked the creature's health down a bit, but not tons. Horc's wolf went after the same defender as Steelmaiden's spectral wolf appeared. For several minutes the sound of heated battle filled the passageway. By the time it was over, the entire party was sweating, panting, and ready to collapse.

"Let me heal everyone before I get my mana back up," Greensleeves said. "Wow, that one was tough."

"Yeah it was." Slasher slumped against the nearest wall and closed his eyes.

"At least we've found the Gnolls," Baladara said. "But did they have to be so bloody strong and so many of them?"

"One of them for each one of us," Steelmaiden said as she knelt to loot. "Almost like the AI controlling the game was counting."

Coins clinked in Horc's pouch. He was too tired to look and see how many of them there were. He'd loosed spell arrows like a madman until he'd run out of mana, then he'd continued to fire special arrows. He pulled out a chunk of meat and tossed it to his wolf to help it mend the damage it had taken in the fight. The wolf curled up at Horc's side as he lowered himself to the floor. Horc hadn't taken any damage but using mana as quickly as he had drained him almost as badly. He took out his flask and drank until his mana was restored.

"This level might take a while," Baladara said. "I almost wish it wouldn't. I'm ready to call it a night. If I gamed this hard every day, I'd be a lot smaller IRL."

"Yeah, I hear you," Greensleeves said as he finished healing Steelmaiden who'd nearly died so many times during the battle that Horc had stopped worrying about her health bar and just fired as many hard-hitting arrows as he could.

Horc laughed. He knew what it would take for Mike…aka Baladara, to be smaller IRL and a couple of nights of hard game play would be just the start of his journey to fitness.

"Hey, don't laugh at me." Baladara glared his direction. "You're not exactly a beefcake model yourself."

"True." Horc shrugged and was thankful the wall was supporting him. "But I don't get many complaints."

"I didn't realize you dated," Baladara's tone softened.

"Haven't in a while." As Horc said it, he tried to remember the last date he'd been on. It had been a long time, and not that memorable. If he survived being trapped in the pod, he'd make an effort to change that. He wanted his life to be more than just work and games, although it would be nice to have someone to game with.

Steelmaiden sighed. "Okay. I'll be the first to admit that my IRL bod isn't as awesome as this." She spread her arms wide and turned around. "But then most of the real players I know aren't. Hell, Baladara, you're not even a real woman, just a guy playing a girl in a game. I know it's a turn on for a lot of guys, but for some of us it's kinda odd."

It was Baladara's turn to shrug. "What can I say, like I told Horc last night, or whenever it was, I don't like looking at guys' bodies. Girls are nicer, so I play a girl."

Slasher nodded. "Before I got a pod, I played girls a lot, depending on the quality of the graphics. But since getting the pod, I don't do it as much. It's too real and feels odd, but that might just be me." He looked to Horc and Greensleeves.

Greensleeves shook his head. "Never tried it, and probably never will. I don't mind looking at guys."

A low growl came from Horc's wolf, making everyone pause and stare down the passageway. Horc and Baladara clambered to their feet. Steelmaiden and Slasher pulled their swords. Seconds later, two Gnoll Protectors came walking around the corner. The party got lucky and there were just the two of them. They were full of steel and magic in seconds and down in less than two minutes. After another quick heal, they continued finding their way through the maze.

"HEY, I think this might be the key for this level," Steelmaiden held up a clear crystal sphere from the corpse of the latest Gnoll Protector to fall to her blade. "It's not showing a quest item, just a crystal orb."

"Might be," Horc agreed. "The others haven't been quest items either, just crystals of various sorts." His hand brushed the pouch he'd put his crystal into.

"We won't know until we find the door," Greensleeves said as he leaned against the wall and drank from his flask. "You know, if we keep having to renew our mana and health after each and every fight, we might not make it out of this dungeon. I thought I'd picked up enough from town, but now I'm wondering."

"I've had a few drops of drinks," Steelmaiden said. "I don't use mana the way you folks do. If someone runs out, let me know and we'll try to keep going."

"Hey, I think this is a trap door," Baladara said from a few feet away.

"A trap door?" Horc walked over and stared at the square of wood in the floor that looked like it should have some kind of hinge mechanism and a latch, but was just cut out of the wood planks.

Baladara tapped on it and below sounded hollow. Rocking back on her heels, she tapped on a spot a couple feet away from the cut out. It sounded like there was something under the boards there. She nodded. "Yep, pretty sure that's a trap door."

Greensleeves looked up and down the section of passageway they'd just turned down. After two dead ends in a row, it was the first open corridor they'd found in a little while. "But we haven't found the boss on this level. If we go down there, we might get stuck and not able to get back." He got a distant look, something Horc recognized as him checking something in his interface. His fingers danced in midair, and he swiped a couple of times. "Yeah, according to the main dungeon quest, we've got two more kills to make. They might both be on the last level, but the way the rest of it has been laid out, I doubt that."

"There might also be treasure down there," Baladara suggested. "Too bad we don't have a thief in the party."

"We haven't run into one yet," Steelmaiden said. "With some of the shifty pricks I work with, I'm a little surprised by that."

"Can't be helped now," Slasher said, kneeling at the door. "Let me see if I can force this thing open. While I do that, why don't a couple of you try tapping rocks in the walls? Maybe one of them releases the door, or something."

Horc nodded and walked to the wall opposite the one Greensleeves was heading to. "We can do that."

"Good." Slasher groaned as he tried to get a purchase on the edge of the wooden cutout. "This might not be easy."

Horc tried to keep track of where he'd been pushing rocks, but it still took them nearly half an hour to find the right rock. The cutout popped up out of the floor and hovered there a couple of feet higher than it had been.

"Magic." Steelmaiden frowned as she tried to move the floating door, but it wouldn't budge. "We might need to split up, leave someone here to make sure the door stays open and the rest of us go check out what's below."

"Shouldn't we make sure it's more than just a small storage spot full of gold first?" Baladara laid flat on the ground, ducked under the door and looked in. "Okay, looks like there's another passageway down here, but it doesn't look like the maze. I bet someone dug this out. Also unless we can find a torch or something else to provide light, I'm going to have to go to illuminate the situation."

"Okay." Horc heaved a heavy sigh. It almost felt like they were being manipulated to go a certain way and do particular things. "Since I know which rock to push, why don't I stay here? Slasher can hang with me. Baladara, Steelmaiden, and Greensleeves check out the passageway. That way if something bad happens, Greensleeves can heal them."

Greensleeves frowned. "And if something happens to the two of you?"

"You'll find the door closed when you get back, and we'll run like hell back to the pit trap," Slasher said. "We shouldn't encounter any mobs back that way."

Steelmaiden huffed. "No, that way might be clear since we haven't been in the maze long enough to have the server reset everything on us. It's not a great plan, but it doesn't completely suck."

"Alright then." Baladara swung her legs over the edge and jumped down. "Let's keep moving."

23

HORC TRIED not to pace. He forced himself to sit against the wall and rest. They were in the middle of enemy territory and he was supposed to be trying not to die. He wasn't sure how he was going to be able to rest.

Slasher sat across the corridor from him. "Man, this is one of the coolest games I've ever played. But then I haven't played many immersive games like this. I was around for the start of VR games, but my wife isn't big into them, so I haven't played much recently."

"I do Galactic Explorers," Horc said. "Similar interface through the pod, but much different game. I do like the total immersion into the game the pods give us."

"Yeah. Really awesome." Slasher grinned. "I know that your pod being buried and all isn't great, but I know that tech guys and developers are watching and recording everything. I don't know what the record for being in a pod is. The things are so new. There's a lot we don't know, even after years of testing. You might help set some guidelines for usage and stuff."

"It would be a lot nicer if I'd known going in that something like this might happen and could've been ready for it," Horc said. "What happens if I die in here? I don't even have a will. Not that I have a lot of stuff, but where will it go?"

"Family, I suppose," Slasher said. "If there's something different that you'd like, let me know and I'll see that it happens."

Horc shook his head, wishing the rock wall was a lot more comfortable as he leaned there. "Would something like that even be legal? Trapped in this game, I don't have any way to make my wishes known."

"I don't know, but it might be worth a try."

Horc's wolf stood and walked over to the hole in the floor where the door still hovered. He looked down and whined.

"Hey, the others might be coming back." Horc stood and hurried over to the floating door. Horc welcomed the idea of something happening. He hadn't liked sitting there waiting and then talking about what would happen if he couldn't get out of the game just made things worse.

Baladara floated up, out of the hole. "Miss us?"

Horc couldn't help but chuckle. "A little."

Greensleeves jumped up and grabbed the edge of the hole so he could pull himself up. "Okay, so we've got a bit of a dilemma now."

"What's that?" Slasher asked as Steelmaiden copied Greensleeves' move to get back up with them.

"We found a way out," Baladara said. "This is the opening for a tunnel that goes to the side of the mountain. You know, up where we found the Gnoll Scouts. If we wanted to, we could leave the dungeon."

Steelmaiden brushed dust off. "Yeah, get out, go grind a while, put on a few more levels and come back and finish the dungeon."

Slasher pursed his lips and shook his head. "How do we even know that would work? The dungeon will most likely reset when the servers do. That would mean starting over."

"Not if we already have the keys." Steelmaiden patted her pouch, where she'd put the orb she'd found earlier.

"If the crystals are part of the dungeon, they might disappear when it resets," Slasher argued. "No, I say we go on. We've just got to finish this damned labyrinth, then get through the final level. We've come this far."

Steelmaiden grinned. "I've got to say, I'm totally with you, but we wanted to make sure you guys were okay with us keeping on keeping on."

Horc frowned. "Sounds like you three had it figured out before you got here."

Greensleeves shrugged. "Not exactly. I've been voting to leave and come back. It is the safer thing to do, but they wanted to continue. We decided to let the two of you be the deciding vote."

Horc frowned harder. "But I didn't get a vote."

"No, but at this point it's three for going on." Baladara crossed her arms and scowled. "If both of you had wanted to leave, we would've, but one of you wants to go on, at least one of you. So, the ones for going on overrule. Isn't democracy great?"

"Yea, but we work for a growing mega corp and we're in a fantasy game they created." Horc argued. "I'm not sure democracy applies at this point. But just for the record, I'd be voting to go on. Sure, it's more dangerous, but where's the fun without a bit of danger?"

Steelmaiden laughed. "I like you, Horc. You've got balls."

He didn't really see much of a choice in the matter, and the more he'd thought about his situation, the more he realized if he hadn't been in the pod, he'd probably have been killed when his house was destroyed. He was lucky, and he might as well enjoy himself while he had the chance. Halfworld might be the last game he ever played.

AS NEAR as any of them could figure, they were near or at the center of the maze when they finally found something other than Gnoll Protectors. Coming down the passageway toward them were three Gnolls. Two of them read **Gnoll Squire, level 13**, and one read **Gnoll Knight,**

level 18. The squires had one star after their names and level, and the knight had three.

Horc pulled his head back around the corner and looked at the others. "We might have trouble." He quickly relayed what they were.

"Then we need to concentrate on the knight first," Steelmaiden said. "If Slasher, the wolves and I all take him on, we might be able to take him out, then see about the two smaller ones. They probably won't be much of a problem. I'll draw all the aggro to myself to keep them focused on me"

"The knight will be an issue," Greensleeves said. "But that's a good play. Horc and Baladara hit them as hard and fast as you can. I'm going to go Tree and save all my mana for healing. Something tells me you guys are going to need it."

Steelmaiden grinned. "You haven't let us down so far."

"Don't jinx it." Greensleeves shook out his hands in prep for casting. Then he shifted form.

Steelmaiden and Slasher stood side by side with their steel out.

"Let's do this." Steelmaiden dashed around the corner and let out her War Cry.

There were shouts from the knight and squires.

Horc unleashed his first volley on instinct. The Impact Arrows had become second nature for his fist attack. Then he stared for a second. He'd never seen Gnolls like the ones they were attacking. The squires weren't too different from the protectors, but they were in chain mail, not leather or cloth armor like every Gnoll they'd seen to that point. The knight made him wonder. The big bipedal canine had on plate armor. It was still agile enough to get under Steelmaiden's first swing, but it couldn't dodge Slasher's blow that followed hers. The big man's sword rang out as it clanged off the knight's canine headpiece, that looked more like a snarling wolf than a Gnoll.

"Keep going, Dude," Baladara urged as she unleashed her first Fireball.

"Oh." Horc shook himself as the squires closed in on Slasher and Steelmaiden. He hit them both with Impact Arrows, then switched to a round of Poison Arrows for all three of them. The squires' health showed damage first. Dropping slightly, but the two didn't turn from their attack on Steelmaiden, who was taking all the damage from the three. Her health was already at half and her spectral wolf was fading away.

Horc did Flame Arrows for his next attack and fell into an easy rhythm of firing, trying to focus more effort on the knight who was dropping bit by bit as everyone's mana dipped with each round.

"Impact Arrows on the squires!" Greensleeves shouted. "I'm out of mana. Getting Steelmaiden a healing potion." He pulled out a potion from somewhere in his bark and ran toward the warrior who was finally able to turn her attention from three opponents to two.

A golden glow hit Horc and his mana restored as he leveled to fourteen. Baladara leveled too.

"Yes." Baladara's hands glowed and she cast a huge Fireball.

Her attack hit the squires at the same time as Horc's arrows. It knocked the two of them back. Greensleeves made it to Steelmaiden and handed her a potion. He pulled out one and rushed it to Slasher.

Horc hit the two Squires as hard as he could with Flaming Poison Arrows. They were down to half health. The potions brought Steelmaiden and Slasher back to three quarters health too.

Steelmaiden did her Battle Rage and was a blur of steel and flowing red hair as she went after one of the squires.

Slasher did a similar move after the other one.

Horc alternated between the two, peppering them with arrows as fast as he could while his wolf stayed next to Steelmaiden, attacking her Squire until the Gnoll dropped to its knees, and then finally to the ground.

With an incredible spinning attack, Steelmaiden lobbed off its head and she, Slasher and Greensleeves all leveled to fifteen.

"Whahoo!" Steelmaiden yelled and laid into the final squire with gusto.

Seconds later, the squire dropped to the ground with a whine and died.

"Wow." Horc panted. "That was altogether too close."

"But man was that fun." Steelmaiden grinned at him.

"That's one way to put it," Slasher said, opening his visor to wipe his brow. "I thought I was a goner. Even with the healing potion, those squires were rough."

"But we did it," Baladara said.

"Here healer." Steelmaiden pulled a staff from the knight's corpse. She flung it at Greensleeves. "I think this is something you can use."

"Yeah." Shifting back to human, Greensleeves smiled broadly as he switched it out with the mace he'd been carrying. "Plus five damage, decrease in casting time for healing spells, plus six armor, and plus twenty on fire resistance. Sweet drop."

"And this." Steelmaiden held up a wand.

"Mine!" Baladara shouted and jumped for it. She took it from Steelmaiden and held it up. "Awesome. Plus three to spell damage, plus one to melee damage, Mini Fireballs every three rounds. Perfect for a mage."

"I think we're all doing pretty good in this dungeon." Slasher pulled out some food and drink. "But we've struggled for every piece of loot and XP we've got. We're doing great."

"And only one more level to go." Horc tossed a chunk of meat to his wolf, who had been knocked down to only a quarter of its health.

Greensleeves stood from where he'd been drinking after getting the staff. "Then let's keep moving. The sooner we get done with this the sooner we can rest."

Horc and the others rose and without another word, headed toward the next turn in the passageway. Horc felt powerful as they walked along. They'd managed to do so much in the dungeon. He felt good about what they'd accomplished. With his friends working together the odds were that they could finish the dungeon. Deep in his gut. He felt sure of it.

24

BEYOND THE fourth door, the narrow corridor was ornately decorated in velvets, silks, and gold inlay. There were various paintings, all of Gnolls with crowns, jewels, and huge weapons.

"Okay, a little unexpected opulence here," Baladara muttered as the party walked along.

Although Horc wasn't sure what to expect in the last level of the dungeon, walking down a hallway that looked like it belonged in a palace, not several stories underground, wasn't part of what his mind had conjured up as they'd traversed the ever-changing landscape of the cave they first entered.

"I guess even Gnolls like to feel important," Steelmaiden said.

"But they don't even talk," Greensleeves stopped and stared at one of the paintings, a piece of artwork that had an almost Picasso feel to it. "How can creatures that don't talk have this level of art?" He shook his head and turned away from the expressionist nightmare that was fractured and drooling all at the same time.

"I think we need to bring this up to the game designers," Slasher suggested. "If they're going to go for this level of realism on this level, they need to work on it all the way through the dungeon." He paused and dislodged a stone from his steel boot. The stone bounced once on the thick carpet and stopped. "I can't remember if the Gnolls outside said anything or if it was all just grunts and howls."

"Just basic animal sounds if I remember right," Greensleeves said. "I'm definitely going to point this out to Rick later. If we're going for a higher level of reality, they might end up needing more monsters saying things and less just growling and drooling."

"If nothing else, hurling insults might be a good idea," Horc said.

They turned a corner and stopped. Two massive Gnolls stood a short distance away guarding a set of large wooden doors. They were dressed in bright purple surcoats with gold striping and floral designs. They each carried huge pikes and shields that were nearly as tall as they were, and each one of them was easily seven feet tall. Bigger and more dangerous than most of the other Gnolls they'd faced. Easily German shepherds when compared to spaniels.

Gnoll Defender, level 18 was in bright letters above each of their heads along with a star at the end.

The party scurried back around the corner.

Horc paused and glanced back, but neither guard had moved.

"We've dealt with worse odds," Steelmaiden said. "I doubt we can pull one of them without the other, so we'd be better off going after both at the same time."

With a slow thoughtful nod, Slasher unsheathed the sword he'd gotten in a recent drop. "I can go right and you can go left. Horc and Baladara can give us support and let's hope the noise doesn't aggro anyone who's behind those doors."

"Good plan." Steelmaiden gripped her axe. "Let's do this."

"Ready." Baladara popped her knuckles and grinned.

"I'm good." Greensleeves said. He'd renewed everyone's buffs before they opened the door in the maze that led to the last level. They were all as good as they were going to get.

With a solemn nod, Horc strung an impact arrow, and at his side, his wolf tensed so much that the fur on its spine rose. They were acting like they'd all been fighting together for a long time. Horc couldn't remember the last time he'd had a party that acted like a well-oiled machine and they'd managed to get there in just a few hours. It was wonderful.

Steelmaiden led them around the corner with an empowering battle cry that wasn't the one she normally used to draw aggro to herself.

Slasher echoed her cry and the Gnolls guarding the door brought their pikes to the ready.

As soon as Horc unleashed his first arrow at the Gnoll on the right, his wolf followed the projectile down the opulent hall. The thick carpet muffled the sound of its footfalls. As the battle was joined, the entire thing sounded wrong. The carpets and tapestries on the walls softened the sound as Steelmaiden swung her axe hard and the blade slid across the guard's shield. There wasn't a sharp clang as Slasher's sword caught the guard's pike. The muted sounds hit Horc hard. It was like the world rebelled against their fighting.

"Your quest stops here!" one of the Gnolls shouted, although the words came out very guttural and gravelly.

"At least these talk." Baladara was working on her second spell, after the Gnoll Steelmaiden had engaged had managed to block her first Fireball with its massive shield.

"Yeah, but they need better voice actors," Greensleeves said as he got his first spell off and the one Slasher fought was suddenly engulfed in thorny vines.

Horc managed to catch Steelmaiden's opponent in the throat with a Razor Arrow. It sprayed blood all over the Barbarian woman. She shouted at it, sounding more like an animal than the Gnoll did. She swung her axe hard as Horc hit the guard again, this time managing to catch it on fire.

The Gnoll howled long and low.

The sound sent shivers through Horc, but his wolf, Steelmaiden, and Slasher all paused in their attacks.

"Crap, that was some kind of stun howl," Baladara said as she got off her next spell. "Hit them as hard and fast as you can. We need to keep them busy until the spell, or whatever that was, cools down."

"Let me see if I can counter," Greensleeves started casting something that made a purple haze around his hands.

Horc didn't need to be told twice. He fired as fast as he could, not really caring which arrows he was pulling form his quiver, just so long as he was hitting one of the Gnolls at the end of the hall.

The guard on the right held his shield up and waded into Horc's stream of arrows. It walked past the three party members who were stunned, but didn't close on the ones doing distance damage.

"To the right two steps." The other one's voice was barely audible from down the hall, but the Gnoll with the shield moved as instructed.

"Shit. Greensleeves do something!" Baladara got off a round of Magical Bolts that glowed purple as they blazed down the hallway.

"Trying." Greensleeves said through gritted teeth as he finished his spell.

Something glowed purple as the Gnoll from the left raised his pike and slashed down at Steelmaiden.

The one holding up the shield blocked part of Horc's view, but he recognized Steelmaiden's shout of anger and the ring of two weapons meeting was unmistakable, even as strangely muffled as they were by the carpets and tapestries.

The guard who had attacked them was pushed backward. Steelmaiden swung her axe at him as he stumbled and tried to regain his footing. She forced the point as Horc stopped firing into the shield and managed to hit the guard while he was off balance.

Steelmaiden kept hitting the guard hard and fast, her axe tearing huge chunks off him as his health bar continued to slide down with each of her and Horc's hits.

Another howl rent the hallway as Horc's wolf shook off its stun and launched itself at the Gnoll with the shield.

"Way to go, Wolf!" Baladara shouted as her next spell got past the shield because the guard had turned slightly to deal with the attack from behind.

Horc and Steelmaiden had her target down to less than a quarter life by the time Greensleeves managed to revive Slasher, who instantly went to work on the one the wolf was savaging as Baladara continued to tear it down slowly with one spell after another.

When Steelmaiden finished off her target, the one with the shield was down to less than half. With their concentrated fire on it, it crumbled to the floor without another word.

Horc's mana was low by the time they were done. Everyone stood quiet for a moment, as if listening for something else to happen, for some other defenders to show up.

"Drink up, folks," Greensleeves said. "We need everyone at the top of their game before we open those doors.

"No problem." Horc tossed his wolf a chunk of meat, then pulled out his flask. The water was cool and refreshing as always. As he drank, his mana recovered all the way up. He glanced at the party's icons on the left of his vision and everyone else was nearly back to full strength too.

"Hey, I think this might be our key." Baladara straightened from where she'd been looting one of the guards after she'd finished off her drink. She held up a yellow star-shaped crystal.

"Unless we find out otherwise, I'd say you're probably right," Greensleeves said. "At least it looks like all the others."

Horc wasn't sure if it was good or bad that they'd found the key so early in the dungeon level. He'd figured it would've dropped from the big boss, the Gnoll King himself. But then he wasn't a game designer.

Steelmaiden hefted one of the guard's pikes. "Pike anyone? I can't use it. It's a pole arm."

Horc looked at it.

Guard Pike

Damage 20

Speed 2

The name was in red. He shook his head. "Can't use it."

"I can use it," Slasher said. "But that speed is just horrible." He picked up one of the shields. "Now this, this I can use, even if it is taller than I am."

"Then take it," Greensleeves said. "I think the way we're racking up gold on this one, we'll all be able to hit the flea market and get better stuff when we get back to town."

Slasher dropped his old shield in his bag and put the new one on his arm. He whacked his sword against it. "Yeah. Definite upgrade."

"We're doing good." Baladara said as she closed her bag and stood. "Now let's finish this off. My real feet are starting to hurt. Sometimes I miss the old days when we could sit in a chair and do our gaming."

Horc laughed. "You'll appreciate it when you start dropping weight." He wondered if he was going to have lost any weight when he woke up and could get out of his pod. He knew a few hours in the pod could be exhausting, and he'd never pushed it beyond six. He knew he had been in game for more than a day. That had to be wearing on his body.

STEELMAIDEN PUSHED the doors open slowly. The inside of the next room was as posh as the hallway had been. It was thickly carpeted; there weren't any chairs or benches in the room, but it reminded Horc of a church sanctuary. There were ornate marble columns, carved with depictions of wolves and Gnolls. More portraits lined the walls that weren't covered in tapestries that portrayed battles between the Gnolls and Humans. The scenes looked to be set in the same mountains as the dungeon was in; in fact, one of them appeared to show the cave they'd entered and then the other tapestries showed the Gnolls subjugating the creatures they'd fought to get through the levels and down to the throne room.

In the middle of the room, on a raised altar, was an axe that was being held aloft by a rocky boulder.

"Okay, is this a twist on the sword in the stone?" Baladara asked as she walked up to the axe in the stone.

"Could be." Greensleeves walked next to her as Steelmaiden and Slasher fanned out. There didn't appear to be anyone else in the room.

"This is weird," Horc said, following Baladara and Greensleeves to the altar. "Why have nothing in this room?"

"Maybe they're still working on it," Baladara suggested.

Greensleeves shook his head as he stopped a couple of feet from the axe. "No, Rick was really animated about the dungeon being super cool and that's why I had to start in the human starting zone. Trust me, I prefer running elves and dwarves to humans."

"Then why's it empty?" Baladara said as she reached for the axe in the stone.

As her fingers started to curl around it, a wave of energy surged out of the axe, flinging all of them across the room. Everyone's health bar dropped by a quarter. The doors into the hallway slammed shut.

Baladara stood up, her health bar was at half. "Okay. Not cool. Definitely not cool."

"Just in case there's trouble, renew one at a time," Greensleeves suggested. "Baladara, you're lowest, you first."

"Sure." Baladara sat where she was and pulled out a muffin from her pack, followed by her flask. "That axe is nasty."

"But do we have to interact with it?" Horc asked, walking slowly back to the stone altar.

"Probably to get through this level and free of the dungeon," Steelmaiden said. "In case you didn't notice, the door's closed."

"And locked," Slasher said after tugging and pushing on the door that he'd landed near. "Unless we figure out how to unlock the door, we're stuck here."

"Puzzle time." Greensleeves strolled over next to Horc and the two of them studied the weapon without getting extremely close the way Baladara had.

Horc spotted a couple of indentations on the handle. "Hey, do you think these look like the crystals should fit in them?" He gestured to the spots nearest him.

"Could be," Greensleeves said. "But how do we put them in there without touching the handle?"

Horc pulled out the blue egg-shaped crystal he still had. "Maybe the crystals will cancel out the power blast."

"That's a possibility," Baladara said, looking from the axe to Horc and back again. "Get your health up to max before we try."

"Go ahead Horc," Greensleeves said. "It's just you and me now."

Horc nodded and pulled out a piece of jerky. He tossed the wolf a piece of meat at the same time. As he slowly chewed the tough salty meat, his health returned to full.

"You know, it's kind of stupid for this thing to hit us like that and then give us time to start over," Steelmaiden said. "You'd think the designers would've been a little better at thinking that one through."

"Maybe they did and didn't expect people to think this thing through," Greensleeves said as he pulled out his own refreshments. "Let's hope we can knock our way through this one. That's my last bit of food and drink."

Baladara nodded. "I wasn't going to say anything, but me too."

"Then I've got my fingers crossed this thing isn't going to knock us on our butts again." Horc took a deep breath and tried to keep his hand from shaking as he moved the crystal into position to line up with the first spot on the handle.

The crystal nearly flew out of his fingers as he got it close to the wood. It clicked into place on the handle and for a second, the whole axe glowed with the same blue as the crystal. It eased slightly upward, like the crystal was causing it to rise out of the rock.

"Well that was a good idea," Baladara said, slowly approaching the axe again. She pulled out the yellow star crystal she'd gotten off the guard at the door. "I wonder if we should risk this one. We haven't found the door it opens yet."

Horc looked at the crystal, then studied the axe shaft. "There's a spot for it."

"Let's put the other ones in first," Greensleeves suggested as he and the other two added their crystals.

With each addition, the axe glowed softly and rose higher, but they all managed to avoid touching the axe when they placed their stones.

"It looks like it's coming out," Horc said. "Let's try your stone. If we're lucky once we finish the dungeon everything will be open and we'll be able to get out."

Baladara handed him the yellow crystal. "Okay, but if we get stuck, I'm just logging out and going home."

"Deal." Horc took the crystal and went to put it in the axe.

Like the other crystals, it was drawn into its spot. There was a soft click, a flash of yellow and the axe blade cleared the stone it had been resting on. The axe teetered for a second and started to fall over. Horc grabbed it to stop it from falling to the carpeted floor. He caught it and lifted it high. A message flashed across Horc's view.

Axe of the Gnoll King
Damage 30
Speed 15
+10 against canines
+10 frost damage
+10 earth damage
+10 fire damage
+10 wind damage
+10 spirit damage
Binds when looted.
Accept Decline

Horc stared at the message. "Wow, this is one bad ass axe. It says binds when looted. Does anyone else want it?"

As he asked, two doors across from the one they'd came through opened.

"Thief! Stop them," shouted someone as three Gnolls charged into the room.

"Just grab it!" Baladara yelled and started her spell.

Horc focused on accept long enough for the axe to flash one last time, then it settled heavily into his hand. He quickly swapped his other axe for the new one, then drew out his bow and started firing.

Two of the Gnolls charging them were more Defenders, but the third one was the **Hallenbeck, Gnoll King, level 22** with three stars.

They were at the altar before Horc could get more than two arrows off. The Defenders were armed with pikes again, but the King had a huge sword. They were moving fast enough, Horc didn't even have time to comment about how much like the Dallas Chief of Operations, Hallenbeck looked like. Like with the other bosses the resemblance was obvious and uncanny.

"Hit them hard!" Steelmaiden screamed right before she did her War Cry.

It was still odd how their opponents would turn from the rest of the party and focus on her when she used her aggro pulling ability. Horc just hoped it wasn't more than she could deal with as her health dipped quickly before a blue glow from Greensleeves' healing spell wrapped around her.

"Take out one of the Defenders," Slasher said, "while she and I focus on the King and other Defender." Without waiting for a reply, he starting slashing at the one Steelmaiden had done the most damage to.

"Let's take it down." Baladara said and started slinging Fireballs and bolts of arcane magic at the other Defender.

Horc fired arrows as fast as he could. These Defenders didn't have shields so they couldn't defend themselves as easily. He set up his regular round of magical arrows doing as much damage as he could.

Greensleeves kept healing as the party members fell too far in their health. By the time the first Defender was down, Greensleeves's mana was at almost a half.

With most of the party focusing on the second Defender, Horc started alternating his arrows between the guard and the king. His arrows didn't seem to really do much to the King, but the Defender was dropping quickly as the four of them hit it hard and fast.

"Steelmaiden, drop back!" Greensleeves shouted. "Let me get the spell finished." His hands blurred in blue, Greensleeves sounded tired.

Doing as he said, Steelmaiden dropped and rolled under the King's attack, making it just out of his range as Greensleeves' spell hit her. Her health was at just over half.

Horc hit the King with a Flaming Impact Arrow. The King burst into flames when it hit.

"Damned magic users." The King turned from Steelmaiden and Slasher who was still working on the other Defender. He started toward Horc and Baladara, with most of his health bar still glowing green.

Horc turned his attention from the Defender and focused on the King who was still under the influence of his Impact Arrow and moving slower than normal. The effect was eerie as the King slowly, deliberately stomped toward him.

With Horc's focus on the King, his wolf also attacked him.

The Gnoll King glared at the wolf as it charged him. "Fowl cur, I am the ruler here." As the wolf leapt at him, the king struck it hard with his sword. The wolf yelped as its health dropped by half.

"No!" Horc aimed for the King's face with a razor arrow. Blood flew as the arrow hit him square in the muzzle.

For the first time the King's health dipped below three quarters.

The wolf rolled, then jumped to his feet and charged back into battle. Blood coated its fur. Growling and snarling, it rushed the King as Horc hit it again with a Flaming Razor Arrow. The Gnoll King grabbed hold of the wolf and slung it across the room as it leapt at him. The wolf shuddered and lay still. On the party list, its avatar blinked and disappeared.

"You son of a bitch!" Horc dropped his bow and whipped out his axe. He knew his job was to stand back and sling arrows at things, but the King had just killed his wolf companion. Horc was going to make him pay, up close and personal.

"Horc, what are you doing?" Baladara screamed as her mana bar flashed red before going out as she hurled her last Fireball.

"He killed my wolf!" With the axe in his hand, Horc coursed with power.

"And he's going to kill you if we don't all work together." Baladara swung her staff hard and fast. A Bolt of Lightning hit the Gnoll King as she struck him with it.

Horc hit the King as hard as he could with the axe.

"You wield *my* axe." The King jumped back with a snarl. "That will not help you this day."

The Gnoll King looked a little afraid of the axe. That fear pushed Horc onward. He could work with that fear. He would kill the King, just as the King had killed his wolf.

As he closed in on the King again, Horc noticed the last Defender go down as Slasher sliced its head off. It dropped to the ground, then Slasher and Steelmaiden rushed toward the King.

The big Gnoll swung his sword at Baladara. It hit her. Her health bar dropped under half.

Horc body slammed the monster, knocking it back away from her.

Steelmaiden and Slasher piled on as Horc hit it hard. The axe blazed blue and an icy blast went out of the blade and into the Gnoll.

The King yelped but managed to push Horc off.

As Horc got to his feet, he realized his thumb had pushed the blue crystal in and the crystal wasn't as brilliant blue anymore. He took a second and glanced at the King's health. It was between three quarters and a half. Horc wasn't sure if the ice attack from the axe had done any additional damage to him or not.

The King shoved Steelmaiden and Slasher away hard, then vaulted back to his feet. He seemed to ignore them as he rushed Baladara again. She tried to block his blow with her staff, but he cleaved it in half. Pent up Lighting lanced out of the staff, as the King cut Baladara in half. The Lightning hit all of them. Horc's ears rang and his health dropped as he somehow managed to keep his feet.

Under the Gnoll King's feet, Baladara shimmered and then vanished.

"Damn you!" Horc charged him, bringing the axe down as hard as he could. He tapped the green stone in the handle. Rocks rained down on the Gnoll King as the Horc's blow caught him in the shoulder. His health dropped again, but not as much as it had before.

The King tried to slice Horc with his sword, but Steelmaiden's steel met his. There was a clang and she shoved the King back.

"You will die like the other female." The Gnoll King slashed at her, but she managed to block his blow.

Horc took the opening and hit the King again. His axe sank deep and blood sprayed up from the wound.

Slasher also managed to get in close and pound away on the canine boss. The Gnoll King shoved Steelmaiden away and then ran Slasher through.

Slasher's health flashed red and then vanished. He hit the floor and disappeared.

"Why won't you die!" Horc hit the Gnoll hard as a blue glow erupted around him. As the glow faded, Horc's health jumped by nearly half.

The King's health was well on the way to a quarter, as he traded blows with Horc and Steelmaiden. Then Greensleeves was also there, hitting the King with his staff.

"Gotta take him down quickly," Greensleeves said as he hit hard and fast. "I'm out of mana."

"Crap." Steelmaiden roared her Battle Rage and suddenly seemed to not take any damage when the King struck her. She was a blur of chain mail and fur as she pounded on the King.

Horc went at his back in an attempt to stay out of her way. He tapped the purple crystal as he hit the Gnoll with all his might. Flames gushed out of the wound and the boss dropped to a quarter of his health.

"Steelmaiden, catch!" Greensleeves shouted and threw a vial at her.

The healing potion flew over her head and crashed to the floor. Seconds later damage started showing on her health bar. The Gnoll King landed several solid shots while she fumbled a blow. Her sword sliced carpet as she lost her balance. Then the Gnoll King landed a mighty blow. Steelmaiden's health went red, then out. As he pulled the sword from her stomach, she disappeared.

"Damn it, this isn't working." Horc hit the clear gem as he cleaved at the king again. Lightning danced along the blade as it entered the King.

The Gnoll howled and jerked away from Horc. His health was finally under a quarter. He slashed at Horc, forcing him backward. Horc tried to parry, but at the last second, the King twisted his blow up and the sword scored deep into Horc's arm.

Horc's health was less than half. He had to focus on the Gnoll. He didn't have the state of mind to pop a potion.

Greensleeves whacked the Gnoll hard in the back of the head with his staff.

The Gnoll King hit him hard right back, driving his sword deep into the Druid. It wasn't a killing blow, but it took nearly half of his health.

"Kill him for us, Horc." Greensleeves cast a healing spell. Its blue aura enveloped Horc. Then Greensleeves launched himself at the King.

The spell took Horc up to full health, but the King finished off Greensleeves.

"It's just you and me now, Ranger," the king sneered. "Better men than you have tried to kill me and failed."

Horc held the axe in front of him. "We've definitely got to work on your dialogue. Too cheesy." He touched the yellow stone and swung the axe. A strange yellow aura surrounded it as it hit the King. It knocked the king back. The King's health bar was flashing orange as he staggered backward.

"You're going down." Horc swung the axe hard. The King's dropped in health again.

The King hit Horc hard, dropping his health by a quarter.

There wasn't anyone else there to help. Horc and the Gnoll King were all that remained. Horc tried to dodge out the king's way, but the Gnoll had a wild look in his yellow eyes and pressed Horc harder than before. Even the blows Horc managed to deflect still dropped his health if just by a couple of points. He hit as hard as he could and the King's health began to flash, but his own was well under a half. He couldn't let up. If he let up for just a second it would all be over.

Something shimmered into existence a few feet away.

"Alan, you really haven't listened to our advice, have you?" Miranda asked.

"Not the time." Horc ducked below the King's slash, then kicked out at the boss, catching him in the stomach and sending him back peddling.

"We thought you'd like an update on your situation." Miranda continued, obviously undeterred by his game situation.

The Gnoll King howled and rushed Horc.

"Can this wait a minute?" Horc braced himself for the boss's attack, holding the axe at the ready to block the blow and hopefully finish off the King. He had his finger on the crystal that had produced fire the last time he pressed it.

"Not exactly," Miranda said, she snapped her fingers and the last dregs of the Gnoll King's life vanished. The boss crashed to the ground at Horc's feet.

"What did you just do?" He had the sudden urge to throw the axe at the woman as she stood there calmly a few feet away in the same gray robes she'd worn the last time he'd seen her. She'd robbed him of the victory, then a gold aura surrounded him and he leveled to fifteen. "You ripped me off."

Miranda cocked her head. "How. The boss is dead. You and your party got the XP for it. When I leave, you can loot it and the others. You get what you wanted."

Was that what he wanted? Horc wasn't sure. He'd wanted the satisfaction of killing the creature who'd killed his wolf and his friends. It had taken so much from him, and she'd ended it with just a snap of her fingers. It wasn't fair.

"You've been risking your life," she sounded like a mother chastising a child. "We don't know if you'll survive dying in game. Total Immersions Systems won't be held responsible if you die of your own stupidity."

Horc sighed. "Look. I can't just sit around a bar and wait for my pod to be rescued and me to get out of it. I need to be doing something and running through this dungeon with my friends was doing something."

Miranda shook her head. "I'm not sure I'll ever understand gamers. I came to tell you that the rescue team has reached your house. They worked, as you requested, in getting to the people in the church first. They saved fifteen lives. Twenty-three people died in there, on their knees hoping for divine protection. It looks like it's going to take at least a day, if not more to get down to your pod. Debris from the church and several nearby houses cover the location your pod's GPS is sending from."

A stab of fear went through Horc. "Can the pod last that long?"

"On battery back up? Maybe. It'll be close. Now, would you please go somewhere safe? Or at the very least if you're going to explore Halfworld, do it in zones that are a couple of levels lower than you are." Miranda disappeared without another word.

Horc glared at the spot where she'd vanished.

Hey, you made it through, Baladara said in their group chat.

Where are you guys? Horc asked as he looked around the room before kneeling next to the body of the king so he could loot it.

We're back at the start of the dungeon. Man I'm so glad this isn't one of those games were we lose all our stuff when we die.

Me too, Greensleeves added.

Horc's heart soared as he chatted with his friends. Seeing them die had hit him hard. Even knowing it was game, it was still hard to deal with. *What about my wolf? Is he there too?*

Companion animals are different than players, Baladara said. *You'll have to bring him back. You should have a spell for that.*

Really? As coins clinked in his pocket, Horc stopped looting and pulled up his character sheet. He studied it for several minutes before he found what he was looking for, a Companion Resurrection spell.

Horc cast the spell as quickly as he could. A pool of gray mist appeared on the ground in front of him. The mist slowly congealed into the body of his wolf. It was translucent at first, then became more and more solid.

"Wolf!" Horc dropped to his knees and hugged his companion. Wolf licked his ear and Horc laughed.

Hey, have those other guys already vanished? Baladara asked. *We've only got the king's cash so far.*

What? Horc straightened and realized he hadn't finished looting all the bodies. *Give me a second.* He pulled out a couple of chunks of meat and threw them to Wolf until his health was restored. Then he worked on looting the bodies, and the big room the king had entered from. Once he was sure there was nothing more to be found, he went through the doorway with the star indention he found in the king's room. The stone fit and opened it just like the others had, even if turning it with it still in the axe handle had been slightly awkward.

25

HORC SAT in front of Caleb Sureshot outside of Sureshot's tent. He'd reported to the Ranger trainer after the party returned to Stone Helm City. It had taken him longer than ever to get his training. He'd gained levels and strength fast, probably due to the difficulty of the dungeon.

"Now, since you stand at the halfway point between two people, it's time for you to experience the other side of yourself," Sureshot said.

"What are you talking about?" Horc asked.

"You're a Half-Orc," Sureshot explained. "So far you've experienced the Human side of your existence. To truly understand existence here on Halfworld, you must understand both halves of yourself. It's time for you to go forth to the Orc lands and experience that side of things."

Horc screwed up his face, trying to understand what his trainer was talking about. "Wait. But I've got friends here. A party I trust."

Sureshot shook his head. "To truly be whole, you must embrace the fullness of yourself. There is no choice for you."

A quest window popped up.

Two Spirits in One Body
Journey to Red Wind Terrace and find Ranger Thunderbow.
Rewards 5,000 XP
Accept—Decline

Horc stared at the quest. It seemed fairly straightforward. It wanted him to leave the human lands, to leave his friends. He wondered what would happen if he declined the quest. Would there be other things for him to do in Stone Helm City? Would he be able to do anything more than wander around and grind on critters until the rescuers got his pod free and saved his life?

At his feet, Wolf whined and lay his head on Horc's knee.

He scratched the shaggy head as he continued to stare at the quest. He wanted to keep seeing what Halfworld had to offer. He didn't have anything better to do until the pod was free and he could return to his regular life.

With a heavy sigh, he accepted the quest.

Sureshot nodded. "You have made the right decision. To totally understand ourselves and our places in the world, we must embrace all aspects of what she has to offer. You have done us a great service here in Stone Helm City by killing the Gnoll King. The rest of Halfworld awaits your coming."

"I guess so." It all sounded a bit deep for Horc. He stood and waved at Greensleeves who appeared to be finishing up with his trainer. They all agreed to hit their trainers and then meet back at the inn before calling it a night. He wondered how he was going to tell them all that he was going to need to go into the Orc lands next. Their party was going to dissolve and they would all be on their own until they had missions come up that would pull them back together. He wasn't sure the game would be as fun without his friends around.

He and Greensleeves walked in silence as they left Druid Park. Horc knew he was going to go on, but he wished he had some clue what was awaiting him in Red Wind Terrace.

Horc's Adventures continue in "The Arena"

If you'd like to stay on top of new releases
and upcoming work by Drew Seren, please join our
mailing list at www.drewseren.com
And if you enjoyed Horc's first adventure,
please leave a review at your favorite bookseller.
It's easy and won't take you very long.

THE NEWB
Drew Seren Bio

Drew Seren was raised on a diet of science fiction, both in print and on the screen. He spent many nights watching Star Trek and Space 1999 with his father. Comic books were a main staple of his reading, and then when he was in high school he started reading *Dragon Riders of Pern* and quickly began devouring any science fiction he could, luckily his father had an extensive library at the time. He started writing soon after that, letting writing help him make it through class. During college and his corporate life, Drew spent a lot of time writing to help him endure the mundane things that gnawed at him. Through his twenties and thirties, comic books and science fiction helped him survive. To this day, he's still reading as much or more than he's writing. He's also an avid gamer, playing first *Dungeons and Dragons*, and currently lots of *World of Warcraft*. He's recently turned his attention to writing full time and exploring the vast galaxy through new and interesting eyes.

Stay in touch with Drew through his website
www.drewseren.com

and Facebook pages
fb.me/drewseren

Feel free to drop me an email
drew@drewseren.com

www.ingramcontent.com/pod-product-compliance
Lightning Source LLC
Chambersburg PA
CBHW071151180726
48291CB00007B/2417